"Speaking of thanks," Kevin said, "I've been meaning to thank *you* for freeing up Elizabeth so I can have a chance with her."

Todd clenched his fists. "Stay away from her, Holmes."

"She's capable of choosing her own friends."

"She doesn't know any better," Todd answered bitterly.

Kevin laughed. "No one around here seems to know any better. What sheltered lives you've all led. But Sweet Valley's not such an idyllic place after all, is it Wilkins?"

Todd frowned. "What do you mean?"

"I thought I was moving to a safe little town. But I hear there was an . . . incident."

Kevin beat up Mr. Caster, Todd thought with disgust.

"I know what you're thinking," Kevin continued. "You think you should turn me in. But you're not going to. And you know why? Because what happened to Mr. Caster could happen to anybody. It could happen to someone you care about."

"No," Todd said hoarsely.

"It *could* happen to someone you care about, Wilkins, but it won't. I know I can trust you to keep quiet." Kevin sneered. "When it comes down to it, we're a lot alike, you and I."

"No!" Todd repeated desperately.

Bantam Books in the Sweet Valley High series
Ask your bookseller for the books you have missed

SWEET VALLEY HIGH

Super Star

TODD'S STORY

Written by
Kate William

Created by
FRANCINE PASCAL

BANTAM BOOKS
NEW YORK · TORONTO · LONDON · SYDNEY · AUCKLAND

RL 6, age 12 and up

TODD'S STORY

A Bantam Book / August 1992

Sweet Valley High is a registered trademark of Francine Pascal

Conceived by Francine Pascal

Produced by Daniel Weiss Associates, Inc.
33 West 17th Street
New York, NY 10011

Cover art by James Mathewuse

ISBN 0-553-29207-2

Published simultaneously in the United States and Canada

Bantam Books are published by Bantam Books, a division of Bantam Doubleday Dell Publishing Group, Inc. Its trademark, consisting
of the words "Bantam Books" and the portrayal of a rooster, is
Registered in U.S. Patent and Trademark Office and in other coun-
tries. Marca Registrada. Bantam Books, 666 Fifth Avenue, New
York, New York 10103

PRINTED IN THE UNITED STATES OF AMERICA

OPM   0 9 8 7 6 5 4 3 2 1

One

"Summer vacation!" Jessica Wakefield exclaimed as she stretched back on her beach towel. "I wish it would last forever."

Jessica's twin sister, Elizabeth, squeezed some suntan lotion onto her arm. "No, you don't," she said. "You'd get tired of it."

Lila Fowler laughed. "*Jessica* get tired of hanging out at the beach, shopping, and going out every single night of the week? Get real, Liz!"

Elizabeth smiled. Lila was right. If anyone could make summer vacation into a career, it was Jessica.

"You should talk, Li," Jessica countered. "You're with me every step of the way. And besides, I'm not going to be a total bum for the entire summer. I happen to have a job."

"Lucky you," Lila said airily. The daughter of one of southern California's wealthiest men, Lila often boasted that she would never have to work for a living. "Anyway, I know all about this Secca Lake day camp counselor thing. It's only for two weeks, and it's probably more play than work. So don't sound like such a martyr."

"I didn't know Secca Lake had a day camp," said Aaron Dallas, the Sweet Valley High soccer star who was in the process of being buried up to his neck in the sand by Winston Egbert.

"It's another new program at the park," Elizabeth explained. "Like the junior ranger program Enid and I were in. It's a two-week day camp for six- to ten-year-olds. The counselors are volunteers from a few different schools, not just Sweet Valley High."

"It's an experiment," added Elizabeth's best friend, Enid Rollins. "If there's enough interest, the park will sponsor the camp on a larger scale next summer."

"Volunteers, huh?" Aaron's girlfriend, Dana Larson, the lead singer of Sweet Valley High's popular rock band, The Droids, watched with amusement as Winston patted the last handful of sand into place to complete Aaron's burial. "What's in it for you if you don't get paid?"

Jessica expressed it succinctly. "A chance to meet cute male counselors."

Dana grinned and winked at Aaron. "Sounds like a good reason to me. But that can't be your motive, Liz."

Elizabeth smiled at her boyfriend—tall, handsome Todd Wilkins. "I've missed working at the park," she said. "It'll be fun to spend some time there again. And I love kids."

"What about you, Wilkins?" Winston asked. "I thought you'd be getting a summer job at your dad's company."

Todd's forehead creased in a frown. Elizabeth knew that her boyfriend's buddies didn't realize what a touchy subject this was for him. "I might. I haven't decided yet," Todd replied nonchalantly. "And camp counseling seems like a good way to start off the summer."

"Basketball must be one of the camp's activities," guessed Maria Santelli, Winston's girlfriend and one of Jessica's fellow cheerleaders.

Todd was a star player on the Sweet Valley High boys' basketball team. "You got it," he confirmed with a grin.

Elizabeth looked thoughtfully at Aaron. "You know, the camp will have soccer, too."

"And they're still signing up counselors," Enid added.

Aaron, almost immobilized by the sand, turned his head stiffly one way and then the other to look at the two girls. "Really?"

"It's something to think about," remarked Dana. "You were just telling me the other day how you miss spending the summer at soccer camp."

"You should sign up," Todd urged Aaron.

"I'm afraid Mr. Dallas won't be able to act as

3

a camp counselor," Winston said solemnly. "You see, what we all feared might happen someday has come to pass. All those school newspaper headlines about what a soccer superjock he is have given him such a swelled head, there's nothing left of the rest of him."

"Maybe *you* should sign up to be a camp counselor," Aaron retorted good-naturedly. "From class clown to camp clown—should be an easy transition."

"It's an idea," said Cara Walker thoughtfully. "I mean, not just for Winston and Aaron. For me, too. I'm looking for something productive to do with my free time."

Cara, a close friend of Jessica's, dated the twins' older brother, Steven, who was a freshman at the nearby state university. Steven lived on campus during the school year, but lived at home in Sweet Valley for the summer. "That's right," observed Jessica. "You've got to fill the hours while Steven's working at the law firm."

Cara laughed. "That's not the only reason!"

"Whatever your reasons, you should all check it out," recommended Elizabeth. "Todd and Jessica and Enid and I are going to have a blast."

"A blast," Jessica echoed. Elizabeth glanced at her twin. She knew Jessica hadn't been kidding about why she had volunteered to be a day-camp counselor. It certainly wasn't because Jessica liked working with kids. Although Elizabeth still enjoyed babysitting, Jessica had no

4

great desire to spend lots of time with young children. But after another year of dating the same old Sweet Valley High boys, Jessica had declared that she was ready for some new faces. "Two weeks is plenty of time to get things started with the man of my dreams," Jessica had told her twin. "And then I'll have the rest of the summer free to enjoy him!"

The twins' different motives for working as camp counselors were typical. On the outside, Jessica and Elizabeth were nearly mirror images of each other. Both were five foot six and slim with sun-kissed blond hair and eyes as blue-green as the nearby Pacific Ocean. But those who knew them well seldom mixed them up, and not only because Elizabeth usually wore her hair in a ponytail and dressed conservatively while Jessica wore her hair loose and dressed in the latest fashions. Each girl's style reflected her distinct personality. Elizabeth was the more serious and down-to-earth of the two. She was just as happy spending quiet time with Enid or Todd as she was partying with the gang from Sweet Valley High. Jessica, on the other hand, was addicted to excitement. Unable to sit still for more than five minutes at a time, Jessica couldn't see how Elizabeth could spend hours each week writing a column for the school newspaper. One thing Jessica and Elizabeth did share, however, was their deep-rooted loyalty to each other.

Elizabeth stood up and brushed the sand

from her legs. "How about a walk?" she suggested to Enid and Todd.

Enid hopped to her feet.

"You guys go ahead," Todd said. "I'm going to help Winston torture Aaron."

Aaron yelped in pretend terror. Laughing, Elizabeth and Enid strolled to the ocean's edge. "It would be fun if Winston signed up to be a counselor," Elizabeth reflected. "I think!" she added with a laugh.

"Never a dull moment when he's around," Enid agreed.

Speaking of dull moments . . . Elizabeth glanced at her friend. She hadn't told Enid one of the main reasons she'd been looking forward to working at the day camp. She could always count on Enid to be a good listener and to offer sound advice.

"Enid, have you noticed anything different about Todd and me lately? About us as a couple?"

Enid raised her eyebrows. "You seem the same as always to me."

"Maybe that's what I mean," Elizabeth replied. "We're the same as always. Since Todd moved back from Vermont, I feel as if we've settled back into our old routine."

"Well, it didn't happen just like that," Enid reminded her. "Remember what it was like when Todd first came back to Sweet Valley?"

"Do I ever," Elizabeth said vehemently. Todd

had been Elizabeth's first love. When his father had been transferred to the Varitronics office in Burlington, Vermont, Elizabeth thought she would never care for another boy again. Then she met Jeffrey French, and for a while she and Jeffrey had dated seriously. When Mr. Wilkins had been named the new president of Varitronics and moved his family back to southern California, Elizabeth was torn between the two boys.

Deciding to break up with Jeffrey in order to resume her relationship with Todd was only the beginning of Elizabeth's difficulties. Todd was back, but things had changed. Now his family lived in a mansion on Sweet Valley's elegant Country Club Drive, and instead of re-entering Sweet Valley High, where he had been one of the best-liked students before his move to Vermont, Todd's parents had enrolled him at Lovett Academy, an exclusive private school.

Initially Elizabeth was intimidated by Todd's new lifestyle, and for a while it had looked as if she'd won him back only to lose him to his new, aristocratic Lovett Academy friends. Eventually, however, Todd made the decision to leave Lovett and return to Sweet Valley High, and things returned to normal between them.

"I remember it all," Elizabeth told Enid. She walked slowly, kicking her feet in the sand. "But I guess I feel Todd and I are getting a little stale. That some of the magic has faded and that we take each other for granted. I'm starting to wonder . . ."

Enid stooped to pick up a shell. She handed it to Elizabeth. "Starting to wonder what?"

"Oh, I don't know. A lot of things. Whether Todd and I have enough in common to last over the long run. Whether we're getting dull because we have *too* much in common." Elizabeth laughed ruefully. "Am I absolutely crazy?"

"No," Enid assured Elizabeth. "Everybody has doubts and mixed feelings at some point in a relationship. Even couples everyone thinks are perfect, like you and Todd! It's just the way life works. Have you talked to Todd about how you feel?"

"A little. Probably not as much as I should, though," Elizabeth admitted. "You know what it's like. We've gotten to the point where we know each other so well, we don't always bother to explain ourselves. I just assume he knows how I feel, and he does the same thing." Elizabeth's face softened. "Maybe I'm being too hard on him, and on us. We've both had to adjust to a lot. I hope I don't sound totally negative. I love Todd more than ever. I should be grateful things feel old and comfortable between us!"

Enid smiled. "You're right, you should be. But it's healthy to recognize that you and Todd need a change in your relationship. Being counselors together at the day camp could be just the thing," she predicted optimistically.

Elizabeth put the seashell to her ear and listened thoughtfully to its muffled song. She hoped Enid was right.

"I feel like Jessica," Elizabeth joked. "A couple of hours at the beach, then a trip to the mall!"

"We're not here to shop till we drop, though," Todd pointed out. "Just to find a birthday present for my dad. I really need your help. I have no idea what to get him."

"What do I get for helping?" asked Elizabeth.

Todd parked the BMW, a gift from his parents, then he leaned over and kissed Elizabeth on the tip of her nose. "How about an ice cream cone?"

"Two scoops?"

"Three if you want."

"It's a deal."

They locked the car and strolled hand in hand across the parking lot to the main entrance of the Valley Mall. "By the way," said Elizabeth, "are you still getting those weird hang-up phone calls?"

Todd frowned. "Yep." The calls were peculiar. They came at all hours of the day and night, and only to the phone number that was listed in Todd's name, not to his family's general number. For two weeks, a day hadn't gone by without at least one call.

"The person never says anything?"

"Not a word," Todd confirmed. "He—"

"Or she," Elizabeth interjected.

"He or she waits to hear my voice and then hangs up."

"Somebody's checking up on you," Elizabeth surmised.

"Seems like it," Todd agreed. "But who and why?"

Elizabeth squeezed his hand. "Maybe you've got a secret admirer," she teased.

Todd snorted. "Well, she's not making points this way."

"She'd better not be!" Elizabeth declared. "She'd better not make points with you *any* way."

"You don't have to worry—about a secret phone caller or anyone," Todd promised lightly.

Even as he spoke, Todd remembered a conversation he'd had with Elizabeth a few nights before. She had told him she was worried they were starting to take each other for granted. *Are we really so used to each other that we don't think about each other anymore?* he wondered. *When was the last time I told Liz how much she really means to me?* He couldn't remember.

Todd stopped abruptly and put his hands on Elizabeth's shoulders. "You don't have to worry," he repeated, seriously this time. "As long as I have you, I don't need anything—or anyone—else. I love you, Liz."

Todd bent his head and kissed her gently.

Elizabeth wrapped her arms around his neck for a quick hug. Then she stepped away and laughed. "The parking lot of the Valley Mall. What a spot for a love scene!"

"I was just trying to be romantic and spontaneous," Todd protested, laughing.

Inside the mall, Todd and Elizabeth paused. "I think we should try Lytton and Brown first," Elizabeth suggested. "They have a great men's department. We're bound to find something for your dad."

In Lytton and Brown, Todd wandered around aimlessly while Elizabeth pointed out items she thought appropriate for Mr. Wilkins. "How about this?" She held up a silver business-card case. "You could have it engraved with your dad's initials."

"He has one already," Todd answered.

Elizabeth pulled Todd over to the designer-tie display. "Well, how about a tie?"

Todd wrinkled his nose. "Ties are just so . . . ordinary."

"*These* aren't ordinary. And besides, an executive can't have too many ties. How about this one? With a gray suit—"

"I don't want to give him a tie," Todd insisted.

"OK, OK." Elizabeth considered for a moment. "How about a pair of pajamas? Or we could always try the bookstore. When I can't think of anything else, I always buy a book."

A tie, pajamas, a book—none of the standard

gift options appealed to Todd. He shook his head.

Elizabeth threw up her hands. "We'll never choose something at this rate! You're being too picky."

"I'm not being picky," Todd replied. "I just want to find the right gift. I want to give my dad something special. Is there anything wrong with that?"

Elizabeth sighed. "Of course not. We'll just have to keep looking. Come on."

They continued their tour of the men's department. Todd knew Elizabeth didn't understand why finding the perfect present for his father, a full month before his birthday, was so important to him. *I'm not sure I understand it myself*, he thought.

One thing was sure. Since leaving Lovett Academy to return to the public high school, Todd had been trying hard to make it up to his father, to please him and connect with him. He knew his parents only wanted the best for him; they wanted him to enjoy the privileges of their new wealth, including the best education money could buy. It had been hard to stand up to them and tell them that in his opinion the best thing for him would be to be back with his friends at Sweet Valley High. Todd was proud of himself for this act of self-assertion, but it hadn't been easy. And he still felt that somehow he'd let his parents down.

"Look at this." Elizabeth pointed to a leather

travel kit. "Your dad could use it on his business trips."

Todd shrugged. "I don't know." He saw the look of impatience on Elizabeth's face. "Tell you what," he said with forced cheerfulness. "I like the book idea. Let's go check out the bookstore."

Elizabeth was only too glad to get out of Lytton and Brown. She marched out of the department store, and Todd hurried to keep up with her.

As usual, the mall was crowded. Todd sidestepped a mob of kids arguing about whether to play video games or go to a movie. Then, out of the corner of his eye, he saw a familiar face.

Todd stopped and turned to stare. He thought he knew him, but from where? Then, just as the young man disappeared into the crowd, it hit him. *Kevin Holmes! It can't be!*

Todd was overwhelmed by a flood of unpleasant memories. There was one thing about his life in Vermont that Todd had never told Elizabeth or any of his other Sweet Valley friends. One night he had been walking home from a basketball game. As he passed through the darkened streets of town, he heard a muffled scream and a scuffle. Peering into an alley between two stores, he'd seen a tall, strong young man robbing an older man.

Knowing that if he yelled the mugger would run away, Todd had dashed to a corner pay phone and called the police. Rushing back to the scene of the crime, he had discovered that the attacker was escaping. He had had no choice. After quickly ascertaining that the victim wasn't too badly hurt, Todd had chased the mugger, tackled him, and kept him pinned until the police arrived.

The attacker was Kevin Holmes, the eighteen-year-old son of a wealthy Vermont businessman. All Todd had known about Kevin was that he was a year ahead of him at Burlington High and that he had been kicked off the basketball team, for what offense Todd didn't know.

Before the mugging Todd had never had personal contact with Kevin, but that changed during the trial. *Although there wouldn't have been a trial,* Todd recalled, *if Kevin's father had had his way.* Todd shuddered with the uncomfortable memory of how Mr. Holmes had approached him and offered him money not to testify against Kevin. Todd had promptly refused Mr. Holmes's bribe, but he had been shocked by the encounter. Mr. Holmes was a prominent citizen in Burlington, a man Todd knew his own parents respected. For a number of reasons, Todd had never mentioned Mr. Holmes's proposition to Mr. and Mrs. Wilkins. He had simply done his duty by testifying to the best of his ability at Kevin's trial.

Kevin was convicted and sentenced to a short prison term. Todd remembered the day Kevin's sentence was announced as clearly as if it were yesterday. Both Todd's parents were with him in court; Kevin's parents were absent. One moment in particular was burned into Todd's memory. As Kevin left the courtroom in custody he'd passed close to Todd. Kevin had paused and given Todd a chilling stare. "I'll get you for this, Wilkins," he'd sworn, his pale green eyes intense.

It can't be Kevin, Todd thought again as he craned his neck to see into the crowd.

"What's the matter?" Elizabeth asked. "Do you see somebody you know?"

"No." Todd took Elizabeth's hand and led her toward the bookstore. "I thought I did for a minute, but I was wrong. Let's go."

It couldn't have been him, Todd told himself one more time. The last time he had seen Kevin, Kevin had been on his way to jail. What would he be doing in Sweet Valley, California?

"I'll get you for this, Wilkins." Again, Todd heard the words and saw the cold look in those light green eyes. He shook his head and tried to rid himself of the crazy thought that Kevin had come to Sweet Valley to make good on his threat of revenge. It wasn't Kevin he had just seen; it was only someone who looked like Kevin.

I'm imagining things, Todd thought. *At least, I hope I am.*

Two

Mr. Wilkins was putting steaks on the grill when Elizabeth arrived at Todd's house the following evening. "I hope you're planning to stay for dinner," Mr. Wilkins said. "This steak right here has your name on it."

Elizabeth dropped her jacket on a deck chair. "Count me in!"

"I gave her a formal invitation," Todd assured his father.

Mrs. Wilkins stepped out onto the patio carrying a basket full of silverware and napkins. "Not that she needs one."

With a smile, Elizabeth took the basket from Mrs. Wilkins and began to set the picnic table. It made her happy to know the Wilkinses considered her part of the family. Her own parents thought of Todd in the same way.

Elizabeth and Mrs. Wilkins went into the kitchen to bring out the salad and bread. When they returned to the patio, Todd and his father were talking about the day camp at Secca Lake.

"Camp starts on Monday but counselor training is the day after tomorrow, Friday," Todd said. "That's when we get our official assignments, but Mr. Schiavitti, the camp director, already told me I'm going to be a sports counselor." Todd's brown eyes sparkled with anticipation. "It'll be fun teaching kids how to play basketball."

"You'll be a great coach," Elizabeth predicted. Todd had just the right personality for coaching: patient, firm, easygoing. "The kids'll love you."

"It'll be good experience," Todd remarked. "A chance to see if coaching is something I'd like to do more of."

Todd's love of sports ran deep. Elizabeth knew he often thought about making a career of coaching or sports management. She looked at Mr. Wilkins, curious to see his reaction to Todd's statement.

Mr. Wilkins flipped the steaks over. His handsome face was impassive. "What are you going to do with the rest of the summer?"

"The rest of the summer?" Todd repeated.

"The rest of the summer." Mr. Wilkins winked at Elizabeth. "After two weeks of playing sports at Secca Lake, you'll be ready to settle down at a *real* summer job, don't you think?" Mr. Wilkins's tone of voice made it clear that he didn't consider being a camp counselor a "real" job.

Todd frowned slightly. "I hadn't given it much thought," he admitted.

"Well, I hope you will," said Mr. Wilkins. "How about interning at Varitronics for a month? A number of departments in the company could use some extra help. Just tell me where you want to work."

Elizabeth supposed Mr. Wilkins wasn't exaggerating. As president of Varitronics, he probably could line up a job for anybody just by saying the word.

"Interning. Hmm," Todd mumbled.

"It would be a chance to get your feet wet in business," Mr. Wilkins continued.

Elizabeth was almost certain Todd wasn't very interested in business. But would he admit that to his father?

"I'll give it some thought," Todd replied in a falsely hearty tone.

"That's my boy." Mr. Wilkins thumped Todd on the back affectionately. "Ready to eat, folks?"

They took seats around the table. When Mr. Wilkins had served the steaks, he turned to Elizabeth. "How about you, Liz? What's your agenda for the rest of the summer?"

"Bert, really," Mrs. Wilkins chastised her husband. "Must everyone have an agenda? Stop pestering them. They're on vacation!"

"I'm not pestering them. And besides, I

know Liz," Mr. Wilkins said. "She's an organizer. A girl after my own heart."

Elizabeth laughed. "I have to admit, I'm taking this summer one step at a time."

"You'd better watch out," Mrs. Wilkins warned. "Or you'll be interning at Varitronics, too!"

Mr. Wilkins shook his head good-naturedly. "OK. I'll stop pestering. I just think there's nothing wrong with planning for the future. When I was sixteen, I was already targeting a career. College is just around the corner, isn't it, son?"

Todd helped himself to some salad. "I'm not in any hurry," he said carefully. "Although I am looking forward to playing college basketball."

"Maybe you'll get a scholarship," said Elizabeth.

"Nothing wrong with a free ride if you can get one," Mr. Wilkins conceded. "Sports certainly have their place. But going to the university on a basketball scholarship doesn't mean you can't major in business."

Elizabeth caught Todd's eye. It was hard to miss what Mr. Wilkins was saying. Sports are fine—for a *hobby*. It was obvious to Elizabeth that Mr. Wilkins wanted his only child to follow in his very successful footsteps in the business world. There was a fine line, though, between parental guidance and outright pressure. And from the tight expression on Todd's face, Elizabeth had a feeling Mr. Wilkins was close to crossing it. Elizabeth waited for Todd to defend his interest in sports, but he didn't.

"It's a little early to declare my major," Todd joked.

"It's never too soon to give it some thought," Mr. Wilkins said firmly. "Nothing's more useful in the long run than a business major."

Todd poked his steak with his fork. "You're probably right."

"I know I'm right," Mr. Wilkins said with conviction. "Pass the salt, would you, Liz?"

Elizabeth glanced sympathetically at Todd. She thought Mr. Wilkins was being unfair to his son. But at the same time she realized Mr. Wilkins would never know what Todd's career interests were unless Todd came right out and told him. Elizabeth busied herself buttering a piece of French bread, and realized that she almost felt a little disappointed in Todd. She remembered what it had been like when Todd first moved back to Sweet Valley and his parents had pushed him to mingle with a more exclusive crowd, and she grew a little apprehensive. Would Todd let himself be steered into a job and career at Varitronics the way he was steered into Lovett Academy and the country club scene? And if he was, would he have the strength to rebel?

By the time dinner was over, Todd couldn't wait to get out of the house and head to the

Beach Disco, where he and Elizabeth were meeting some of their friends, including Winston, Maria, Aaron, and Dana. Aaron and Winston had announced that they had snagged the last two counseling positions at the Secca Lake day camp.

"Sorry my dad gave you the third degree about your summer plans," Todd said to Elizabeth as they climbed into the BMW.

"I take it that's been a big topic lately," Elizabeth guessed. "*Your* plans for the summer, I mean."

Todd steered the car onto Country Club Drive. "You're not kidding. He never used to care how I spent my vacation. But now that I'm old enough to work—"

"Old enough for a *real* summer job," Elizabeth added.

Todd's laugh was humorless. "Yeah, a *real* job. Now that I'm sixteen, he's all over me. I mean, I know he just wants the best for me. He wants me to make the most of my opportunities."

Elizabeth pushed a strand of windswept hair back from her face. "But you can't let him dictate your future for you."

"I don't think he's trying to dictate my future," Todd braked the BMW at a light in downtown Sweet Valley. "He's just suggesting one possible course."

"He's more than suggesting," Elizabeth declared, her eyes flashing. "You said it yourself:

22

he's all over you. You have to stand up for your own opinions!"

Todd bristled. "I always stand up for my opinions!"

Elizabeth reached over and touched his cheek. "I know you do, as a rule," she said, her tone conciliatory. "But you didn't just now. Unless you *do* want to work at Varitronics this summer."

Todd turned his head away from Elizabeth's touch. She dropped her hand. "It's not as easy as that, Liz," he said in a clipped voice. She just didn't understand. She wasn't an only child, with the whole burden of her parents' expectations resting on her.

You don't understand. Todd didn't have to say it out loud. The unspoken words hung in the air between them.

"I know my family situation is different," Elizabeth said. "My mom and dad have three kids to fuss over. And sure, they try to guide us. Steven's working at a law firm this summer and obviously my dad's thrilled that his son might want to be a lawyer, too. But he didn't push it, and he didn't argue when Steven decided to work at a firm that specializes in a different kind of law from the kind dad practices."

Todd shrugged. "Good for Steven."

Elizabeth raised her eyebrows. "All I'm saying is that you'd better watch out if you don't want to get roped into a job you're not going to be happy doing."

"I guess that's my problem," Todd remarked coolly.

"I'm only trying to help!"

"Let's just forget about it, OK?"

"If that's the way you want it," Elizabeth said quietly.

They stopped at another intersection and Todd stared straight ahead without speaking. Elizabeth remained silent as well.

A cluster of people had been waiting on the curb for the light to change. Now they crossed the street in front of the idling BMW.

It was already dusk, but the streetlights enabled Todd to see the faces of the pedestrians clearly. And this time there was no doubt about it. The well-cut sandy brown hair, the light eyes, the sharp, handsome profile, the confident swagger . . .

Todd stiffened, his hands gripping the steering wheel. Kevin Holmes was here in Sweet Valley.

The light changed. Todd hit the gas and roared through the intersection. He wanted to get away before Kevin had a chance to recognize *him*.

Elizabeth stared at Todd, her blue eyes wide with concern. "What's wrong? You look as if you've seen a ghost!"

Todd *felt* as if he'd seen a ghost. For a split second, Todd considered telling Elizabeth about Kevin. Then he decided against it. There was no point in worrying her. He might never run into Kevin again. Unless Todd was the reason Kevin was in Sweet Valley. . . .

Todd forced a smile for Elizabeth's benefit. "It's nothing," he said. He could hear the false note in his own voice, and he knew Elizabeth heard it, too. He knew she thought he was shutting her out for the second time that evening.

Elizabeth looked at Todd, her eyes searching his face for clues. "Remember what we talked about the other day?" she asked. "Well, this is the kind of thing I'm worried about. We need to keep sharing in order to keep things fresh. We need to communicate. We can't get lazy with each other. OK?"

Todd nodded. He knew he should say something to Elizabeth, if not about Kevin then about anything, to show her he shared her concern about their relationship. But right now Kevin Holmes was the only thing Todd could think about.

An uncomfortable silence stretched wider and wider between them. After a while Elizabeth shrugged and turned away.

Kevin Holmes is in Sweet Valley. Suddenly, Todd had a strange suspicion. Those hang-up calls he'd been getting for the past two weeks— Elizabeth had remarked the other day that it was as if someone were checking up on him. Could it be Kevin? No, Todd reasoned as he turned the BMW onto the road that led to the shore and the Beach Disco. It was unlikely. Or was it?

Try as he might, for the rest of the evening Todd couldn't shake the feeling that it was no coincidence Kevin Holmes was in Sweet Valley.

Three

At 7:45 on Friday morning Todd tossed a duffel bag packed with swim trunks, a beach towel, and a couple of clean T-shirts in the back of his car. Several minutes later he pulled into the Wakefields' driveway. Elizabeth, Jessica, Enid, and a bag of blueberry muffins were waiting for him.

Elizabeth smiled at Todd as she slid into the passenger seat. Her bright blue eyes sparkled in the morning sun. Leaning over, Todd brushed her lips with a light good-morning kiss.

"We're carbo-loading in preparation for a rigorous day of counselor training," Elizabeth explained as she took a muffin and then offered the bag to Todd.

Todd laughed. "Hey, you don't have to make excuses to me. I'll take one of those."

Back on Calico Drive, Todd pointed the car in the direction of Secca Lake. He glanced in the rearview mirror and saw Jessica stifle a yawn. "I'm not sure I like this," she said grumpily. "Getting dragged out of bed at the crack of dawn. It's as bad as being in school!"

"I love being up early on a beautiful day," Elizabeth exclaimed. She rolled down her window, letting the fresh morning breeze ruffle her hair.

Jessica yawned again. "I know you do. Which is why sometimes I really don't believe you and I are related."

"You'll wake up when we get to the park," Enid predicted. "They're going to keep us on our toes. Particularly you, Todd. You're a sports counselor, right?"

"Yep," Todd confirmed.

"I'm hoping for sunbathing counselor myself," said Jessica. "Or nap-time counselor."

"I think these kids are a little bit old for nap time," her twin remarked.

"You're never too old for nap time!" Jessica declared.

After a few minutes on the highway, Todd turned onto a side road. Soon he could see Secca Lake sparkling through the trees. Later in the morning the popular recreation area would be packed with people picnicking and swimming. Now there were only a dozen cars in the parking lot.

Todd parked and the four friends walked

across the parking lot in the direction of Secca Lodge. Todd lightly swung Elizabeth's hand.

"Look," Jessica exclaimed as she pointed at a Honda with a Big Mesa High School sticker on its bumper. "As I recall from the last time Sweet Valley High played them in football, Big Mesa has some gorgeous guys."

"You cheerleaders must get a pretty good view," Enid surmised.

"You bet!"

The camp counselors were gathering at the front entrance of the lodge. Todd waved at Aaron and Winston. Jessica was too busy elbowing Elizabeth to greet their friends. "Check *him* out," Jessica commanded. "I knew I was going to like camp counseling!"

Elizabeth followed Jessica's gaze; so did Todd. Beyond Winston and Aaron, three boys and two girls, none of them Sweet Valley High students, stood chatting. Todd glanced briefly at the boy Jessica had noticed, and then he did a double take. Was it possible? Todd didn't want to believe his eyes. The object of Jessica's admiration was none other than Kevin Holmes!

Todd had tried to forget about spotting Kevin two days before. This time, however, he couldn't forget or run away. He and Kevin had come face to face. It looked as if Kevin was going to be a counselor at the day camp!

At that moment, Kevin glanced in Todd's direction. Todd stiffened, prepared for a look of bitterness. He remembered the last time he'd met Kevin's eyes, the day of the sentencing in Vermont.

Kevin's pale green eyes slid across Todd's face, but his amiable expression remained unchanged. Kevin showed absolutely no sign of recognizing Todd.

The twelve camp counselors gathered and sat down in a circle on the grass. Kevin sat directly across from Todd and proceeded to check out the other counselors in a friendly fashion. Once more he looked right past Todd as if they were strangers. It was eerie. Todd couldn't help but wonder if he had made a mistake. Maybe this boy wasn't Kevin Holmes after all. Maybe it was just somebody who looked exactly like Kevin Holmes.

A tall, athletically built man with a sunburnt nose whistled to get the group's attention. "I'm Jim Schiavitti," he announced in a booming voice, "the camp director." He turned to a college-age girl sitting next to him. "And this is Sarah Schmidt. Sarah's studying forestry at the university. She'll supervise the nature counselors and the arts-and-crafts counselors. I'll work with the rest of you. Give a wave when I call your name so we can start getting to know one another." Mr. Schiavitti read from a list on his clipboard. "Jill Blake and Kyle O'Brien from Big Mesa High and Cara Walker from Sweet Valley will be in charge of swimming and water games. All three nature counselors are from Sweet Valley High: Aaron Dallas, Enid Rollins, and Elizabeth Wakefield. Ed Ambrose and Melissa Milliken from Fort Carroll and Winston Egbert from Sweet Valley will be running the arts-and-crafts activities." Mr. Schiavitti looked up, caught Todd's eye, and grinned. "Todd Wilkins and Jessica Wakefield from Sweet Valley and Kevin Holmes, who recently moved to California from the East Coast, will be sports counselors teaching basketball, volleyball, and soccer."

Todd managed to return Mr. Schiavitti's smile, but just barely. There was no longer room for even a shadow of a doubt. Not only was Kevin Holmes a fellow counselor, but he would be working closely with Todd.

"Now, how about some introductions?" Mr. Schiavitti suggested.

Melissa, who was sitting on Mr. Schiavitti's other side, spoke up first. Todd couldn't concentrate on a word anyone said, until Kevin spoke. *What's Kevin going to say? "I'm here to track down Todd Wilkins. I'm out for revenge"?*

Kevin tossed a lock of sandy hair out of his eyes and flashed a disarming grin. "I just graduated from high school." He paused before adding, "In Burlington, Vermont."

"Todd went to Burlington High for a while," Elizabeth exclaimed. "Did you two know each other?"

Todd opened his mouth, but Kevin spoke before Todd had a chance to. "We were at the same school," Kevin replied smoothly, "but we

31

didn't know each other. Wilkins, huh?" He appeared to think it over. "Yep, I remember the name. Basketball, right?"

Todd nodded dumbly, completely taken aback by Kevin's charade. He didn't know what else to do but go along with it. "Right."

"I'm taking some time off before college," Kevin continued without skipping a beat. "Exploring different options, you know? I decided to try southern California for a while as a change from New England." His face creased in another charming smile. "So far, I love it!"

"We're glad to have you on board," Mr. Schiavitti said heartily.

The introductions continued. Todd was so preoccupied, he didn't notice when his own turn came. Elizabeth elbowed him to get his attention. He introduced himself in a few terse words, then lapsed back into confused speculation. What was going on? It was clear Kevin was making a great first impression, coming across as clean-cut and friendly. Where was the dark, angry young man Todd had run up against in Vermont?

Todd studied Kevin's face as Winston introduced himself. Kevin's light eyes crinkled in a good-natured grin at Winston's jokes. Todd shook his head. He'd gone along with Kevin's story and he supposed he should continue to do so. *It's not for me to say anything about Kevin's past to the others*, he decided. He would keep his knowledge to himself; it was the fair thing to do. The other counselors could get to know Kevin and judge him for themselves.

Besides, what people don't know can't hurt them. Todd recalled Mr. Holmes's bribe. He didn't regret never having told anyone about it. It would only have injured or embarrassed people—his family, Kevin's family, even Kevin himself.

Todd wished he could see into Kevin's brain and heart. All he could see, though, was a handsome, laughing face. Had Kevin changed? And was the fact that he was in Sweet Valley, working at Secca Lake for the summer, just an amazing coincidence?

Todd had no way of knowing. But he'd always believed in giving people the benefit of the doubt. He was willing to do that for Kevin; especially since it seemed to him that he had no other choice.

When Mr. Schiavitti announced a break at noon, Elizabeth and the other counselors collapsed on the grass by the lake and dug into the lunch the camp provided. It had been a busy morning. They had taken a tour of the park and rehearsed some water-safety exercises. Then they did some role-playing, acting out problem situations that might arise with the young campers. After lunch they would break up into groups and plan activities for the first day of camp on Monday.

"I'm enjoying this," declared Winston, chomping into an apple.

Jessica rolled her eyes. "If you ask me, Egbert, you'd make a better camper than counselor."

Elizabeth laughed. During the role-playing Winston had stolen the show by playing a Dennis-the-Menace type of kid who'd climbed a tree and refused to come down. Elizabeth took a sip of apple juice and leaned against Todd. He put an arm around her automatically. "This is going to be fun, isn't it?" Elizabeth said. "Todd?"

Todd had been staring into space. Now he blinked. "What?"

"Fun," Elizabeth repeated.

"Fun. Yeah, it is," Todd agreed vaguely.

"You and Jess and Kevin will have a good time together as sports counselors," Elizabeth predicted. "Kevin seems like a really nice guy."

"Umm."

At that moment Mr. Schiavitti tossed a basketball in Kevin's direction. Kevin jumped up and started to dribble the ball on the asphalt basketball court adjacent to the lawn where the counselors were lounging. Then he stepped back to the foul line. He shot twice, making one basket and missing the next. He grinned at Todd. "Want to try your luck?" he called out in a light-hearted challenge.

Elizabeth felt Todd flinch. For an instant she thought he was going to remain seated. Then he got slowly to his feet and walked out to join Kevin on the court. Kevin bounce-passed the basketball to Todd. Todd took his place at the foul line and took aim. He made one basket, two, three. Then he missed twice in a row.

"Should have quit while you were ahead," Kevin quipped as he grabbed the ball. *Swish.* Kevin made five foul shots in quick succession; the ball didn't touch the rim of the basket once.

Aaron whistled in admiration. Jessica clutched Elizabeth's arm. "He's awesome," she breathed ecstatically. "Look at the muscles in his arms!"

Elizabeth was too busy looking at the expression on Todd's face to appreciate Kevin's muscles. Smiling, Kevin bounced the ball to Todd. Not smiling, Todd passed the ball back to Kevin instead of taking another turn.

"It's a tough call," Mr. Schiavitti observed. "I was going to put you in charge of basketball, Todd, but it looks as if we've got two hot shots."

When lunch was over the nature and arts-and-crafts counselors went off with Sarah while the sports and water-games group stayed with Mr. Schiavitti. Elizabeth, Enid, and Aaron decided that on Monday they would start the campers out the way they had started out themselves—with a walking tour of the park trails.

"We can move on from there to bird-watching and plant identification," Elizabeth suggested.

"And bug collecting," Aaron added, a mischievous gleam in his eyes.

The day of training ended at five o'clock. While the counselors changed into swimsuits, Mr. Schiavitti fired up the coals on the grill. Before long, burgers and hot dogs were sizzling.

After cooling off with a swim, some of the Sweet Valley High gang sprawled out on their beach towels. Elizabeth gazed out at the lake. Kevin was in the water with Jessica on his shoulders, playing volleyball with Melissa, Kyle, Ed, and Jill.

"It looks as if Jessica's already getting started on a summer fling," Enid commented.

"Can you blame her?" asked Cara. "Kevin is as sexy as they come." She flashed a playful smile at Elizabeth. "Not as sexy as Steven, of course!"

Elizabeth laughed. "Don't worry. I won't snitch to my brother."

"You girls are so superficial," Winston remarked. "What matters is that Kevin's an excellent guy. He's almost as funny as I am!"

"He's funnier," Aaron claimed. "Friendly, too."

"Too bad you didn't know the guy when you were in Vermont, Todd," Winston said. "He probably could have shown you a good time."

"I managed without him," Todd replied dryly.

"Don't you like Kevin?" Elizabeth asked.

Todd shrugged. "He's all right."

"You're just sore because he beat you out in that little foul-shot contest," Aaron joked.

Elizabeth expected Todd to answer good-naturedly. Aaron was only kidding around; none of Todd's friends really thought he was a poor sport. To Elizabeth's surprise, though, her boyfriend remained silent.

"Come and get it!" Mr. Schiavitti called.

Enid, Cara, Winston, and Aaron jumped up and raced over to the grill. Elizabeth and Todd remained seated for a moment longer. Elizabeth looked up into Todd's eyes. He returned her gaze. "Liz, about Kevin . . ."

"What about him?" she asked, curious to know why Todd was responding so strangely to the new boy.

"He's . . ." Todd hesitated. "He's a good guy," he finished.

Elizabeth knew Todd had started to confide something to her, then had changed his mind about it.

Before she could press him further he got to his feet. Elizabeth trailed him to the grill. She was troubled by Todd's reticence, by the uncomfortable feeling it gave her that she and Todd were somehow out of sync. It was a feeling she'd been getting a lot lately.

We always used to be so in tune with each other, Elizabeth thought as she topped her hamburger with lettuce and tomato. They used to share everything, or if they were silent it was the silence of mutual understanding. This was something altogether different. What was happening to them?

*　　*　　*

The sun was setting over Secca Lake. Todd was halfway to the parking lot with Elizabeth, Jessica, and Enid when he remembered he'd left his beach towel behind. "Go on. I'll catch up," he told the others.

Todd jogged toward the lake. The towel was draped over a tree branch; Todd grabbed it and slung it around his neck. Then, turning to head back to the parking lot, he bumped into someone who'd come up quietly behind him.

It was Kevin. "Nice evening," Kevin remarked, rocking back on his heels and smiling.

The smile gave Todd a chill. It was a different smile than the one Kevin had been flashing all day. There was no warmth in Kevin's expression now; his light eyes were as cold as ice.

It was the first time Todd and Kevin had been alone that day. Todd had no desire to prolong the encounter. "Hmm," he grunted, moving to step around Kevin.

Kevin blocked Todd's path. "One more minute of your time. I just wanted to let you know I appreciate your keeping quiet so far about our previous acquaintance." Kevin paused. "And I *won't* appreciate it if you don't stay quiet. Know what I mean?"

"What happened in the past doesn't have anything to do with now," Todd said cautiously.

"It doesn't, huh?" Kevin laughed sardonically. "I can still thank you, though, for giving

38

me a chance to experience the joys of prison. You're a real pal, Wilkins."

Before Todd could respond Kevin spoke again. "You know, we didn't really get to know each other very well in Burlington." Now Kevin's tone was almost friendly. "I mean, I think you knew more about me than I knew about you. But since I moved to Sweet Valley, I've learned all sorts of things. Like where you live, where your dad works. And that cute blonde, the twin who wears her hair in a ponytail. Your girl-friend, right?"

Todd tensed.

Kevin smiled again. "I'll be seeing you, big guy." He disappeared into the shadows.

For a long moment, Todd remained rooted to the spot. The damp beach towel felt cool against his skin; his face was hot with sup-pressed anger—and something resembling fear.

Kevin's words had been innocent enough, but his veiled threat wasn't. He'd made it per-fectly clear that he was watching Todd, and that his motives weren't friendly.

So much for giving him the benefit of the doubt, Todd thought grimly as he started toward the parking lot. Spending time in jail hadn't brought Kevin Holmes back to the straight and narrow. On the contrary, Todd had a feeling it had pushed him even further off the path.

Four

It was late Monday afternoon. The first day of the Secca Lake day camp was over and it looked as if the program was going to be a big success. Almost one hundred six- to ten-year-olds had enrolled. The campers rotated through various activities during the course of the day, and also participated in many all-camp activities. Each counselor was responsible for a cluster of eight campers. Each cluster was identified by a theme bird or animal and wore a special T-shirt. Todd was in charge of the Eagle cluster, a rambunctious group of eight- and nine-year-olds. As he watched the children toss around a Frisbee while waiting for their rides home, Todd couldn't believe how much energy some of the Eagles still had. *I need a long, hot shower,* he thought. *Maybe even a nap!*

Todd's attention wandered away from his Eagles for a moment. He looked past Elizabeth's Sandpiper cluster and Jessica's Pumas toward the spot where Kevin and his Otter cluster were gathered.

A car had just arrived for some of the Otters. The children took a reluctant leave of their counselor. As soon as the car pulled away, the remaining Otters jumped on Kevin and a free-for-all wrestling match ensued. Todd couldn't deny that Kevin was great with the kids. He roughhoused with them, but in a controlled way: he made sure nobody got hurt. Kevin seemed to really like the kids, and the kids loved Kevin.

It wasn't just the kids, either. The camp's director and the other counselors were wild about Kevin. And the more people fell for Kevin, the more uncomfortable Todd became. *I'm the only one who knows Kevin's true character*, Todd thought as he packed a couple of Eagles into a crowded station wagon. *Or do I?* Todd wondered.

Todd sat down on the grass and watched the remaining two Eagles play Frisbee. On the one hand, Kevin had a criminal record. Todd was pretty sure nobody, not even Mr. Schiavitti, knew that. And Kevin had committed a violent crime: he had robbed an old man and knocked him to the ground. Kevin might still be a menace.

On the other hand, Todd had no hard evidence that Kevin wasn't reformed. *Maybe I'm overreacting*, he thought. It was possible that the conversation they'd had on Friday afternoon was innocent. It was only natural for Kevin not to want Todd to reveal the secret of his past, and Todd supposed it was also natural that Kevin should feel some hostility toward him. That didn't necessarily mean Kevin still harbored a tendency toward violent behavior. But was there any guarantee? Todd sighed heavily. He simply had no way of knowing. He wanted to be fair to Kevin, but he also wanted to be fair to himself and to everybody at the camp, especially the children.

The Otter cluster had all gone home. Todd looked on as Kevin said goodnight to Mr. Schiavitti and Sarah, chatted flirtatiously for a moment with Jessica, waved to Elizabeth, and then headed to where his black Mazda was parked.

As he watched Kevin pull out of the parking lot, Todd knew where he had to go for advice. His friends didn't know about the mugging in Burlington and maybe they'd never need to know. But his parents had shared the experience with him. Todd had been putting off telling his mother and father that Kevin Holmes had turned up in Sweet Valley. They'd been very disturbed by the incident in Vermont and he hadn't wanted to worry them further. He had hoped he could handle this dilemma on his own, the way he'd handled Mr. Holmes's bribe. But this time Todd needed his parents' feedback.

I'll tell them about my conversation with Kevin, and maybe even my theory that Kevin is the one making the hang-up phone calls, he determined. *They'll help me decide whether or not to tell Mr. Schiavitti about Kevin's record.*

Shouldering his bag of sports gear, Todd joined Elizabeth, Jessica, Winston, and Aaron, who were standing in between Todd's glossy new BMW and Winston's careworn VW bug.

"How does the Dairi Burger sound to you?" Aaron asked Todd.

Winston leaned against Jessica, pretending his knees were too weak to support him. "I need to refuel immediately," he announced.

"I think I'll pass," Todd said.

"Are you sure?" Elizabeth sounded surprised and a little disappointed. "A whole bunch of people will be there—Olivia, Ken, Dana, Maria."

Todd brushed her cheek with a kiss. "I'm kind of beat, and my mom's probably made a big dinner. I'll call you later, how about that?"

Elizabeth looked deep into Todd's eyes. She knew his mother's having made a special dinner wasn't the real reason he didn't feel like going to the Dairi Burger with the gang.

But Todd wasn't at liberty to tell Elizabeth Kevin's story—not yet, anyway.

As he drove home alone Todd wished he had gone to the Dairi Burger after all. All through the hectic day he'd been worrying so much about Kevin, he'd completely forgotten about the tension at home. Todd wasn't one hundred percent sure he wanted to talk to his father about Kevin after all. Lately it seemed he couldn't talk to his father about *anything* without it turning into a debate about Todd's plans for the rest of the summer—and the rest of his life.

Over the weekend they'd had another conversation about the possibility of Todd working at Varitronics when camp was over. Only this time, without Elizabeth and Mrs. Wilkins to act as a buffer, the conversation escalated into an argument. The night Elizabeth had come over for dinner, Todd had gone along with his dad's suggestion primarily to keep the peace. But when he had been alone with his father, he hadn't been very diplomatic.

As he turned onto Country Club Drive, Todd heard his own words again in his head. *I just don't know, Dad. I don't know if I want to work at Varitronics or any place like it, this summer or ever! I'm not interested in business. I'm interested in sports.*

Mr. Wilkins, who'd been somewhat warm and encouraging up until that point, had suddenly grown cool. Todd had felt terrible knowing he'd hurt his father's feelings. "You just don't seem to recognize the value of the opportunities you're privileged to possess, Todd," Mr. Wilkins had said sadly.

Finally Todd had given in, again, by promising to give the idea further consideration. But the more he thought about it, the less it appealed to him. *Me, at Varitronics?* The idea simply didn't make sense.

Todd's mother had dinner ready by the time he had showered and changed. Mr. Wilkins, home early for a change, joined them. "I thought you'd be starved," Mrs. Wilkins said to Todd as the family sat down at the dining room table. "So I made a double batch of fettucine Alfredo."

"I am starved and it smells fantastic," Todd said. "Would you pass the parmesan, please, Dad?"

Mr. Wilkins presented the cheese to Todd with a flourish. Todd could tell his father had had a good day at work. *Better take advantage of Dad's mellow mood,* he decided. He sampled the fettucine Alfredo and gave his mother the thumbs-up sign. Then he took a deep breath. "You'll never guess who's turned up in Sweet Valley as a counselor at the day camp: Kevin Holmes!"

Todd expected surprised gasps. Instead, Mr. Wilkins nodded, unperturbed. "Your mother and I were just talking about him. I spoke with a former Varitronics colleague in Burlington today, and he told me Kevin had moved out here."

"Well, you can imagine how I felt when I first saw him," Todd continued, relieved to be unburdening himself. "I was pretty shaken. I mean, Dad, the last time we saw Kevin, he was on his way to jail! I never thought I'd lay eyes on the guy again. I didn't *want* to lay eyes on him. In fact—"

Mr. Wilkins interrupted his son. "Then you'll be interested to hear what Ned had to say. Ned Rolleri from Varitronics Burlington is a close friend of Kevin's father, Harry Holmes. Well, according to Ned, Kevin's made a real turnaround. He's come to southern California to make a new start. All by himself, so he can prove to his parents he's a responsible adult. Isn't that great?"

"Great?" Todd repeated in amazement. He wasn't sure he'd heard his father correctly. How could Mr. Wilkins talk so casually about Kevin? How could he accept his colleague's testimony so easily? Mr. Wilkins had been in court with Todd. He'd heard Kevin's threat.

"Don't you remember what Kevin said to me after the trial?" Todd asked his father. "He told me he'd get revenge for my having testified against him. I don't get the feeling that Kevin's changed. If you ask me, he's not in Sweet Valley to make a new start. He's here to—"

"Now, son," Mr. Wilkins interjected. "I hope you'll give Kevin a chance to prove himself. We know all about the mistake he made, but it's not fair to hold the past against him. I expect you to be bigger than that."

Todd stared at his father. *A mistake? Kevin assaulted and robbed an old man and Dad calls it a "mistake"?*

"After all, Kevin comes from a good family," Mr. Wilkins went on. "He took a wrong turn, but now that he's back on the right track, I'm sure he'll stick to it."

Todd bit into a piece of garlic bread, but he didn't taste it. He could have told his father something about Kevin's "good family." Maybe Mr. Holmes was respected in the Burlington business community, but the fact was that he'd offered Todd a bribe not to testify against his son.

Todd looked down at his plate. He hadn't told his parents about the bribe because he didn't want to worry them. And he'd figured the fewer people who knew about Mr. Holmes's dishonesty, the better. It had even occurred to Todd that the revelation might hurt Kevin in some way; Kevin had enough to deal with, going to jail for his crime. At first Todd had been stunned by Mr. Holmes's bribe. Afterward he wanted to rationalize it. Maybe Harry Holmes had acted out of love, maybe he was desperate to protect his son at any price. But Mr. Holmes had been cold and calculating; the only emotion he'd displayed was a chilly, controlled anger when Todd refused his money.

Now Todd recognized that by not revealing the attempted bribe to his parents, he'd made it impossible for them to see the Holmes family from the same perspective he did. His father still considered Mr. Holmes a fine, upstanding citizen. *Dad thinks Kevin comes from a good family,*

Todd thought. *But it's not necessarily a good family. Just a rich one.*

Mr. Wilkins didn't appear to notice his son's weighty silence. "You know," he resumed as he helped himself to salad, "working at the day camp together might turn out to be a good thing for both of you boys. In fact, I hope you'll make a special effort, Todd. Kevin probably needs a boost. He's a long way from his family and friends and I imagine he doesn't know many people in the area yet."

Todd was more confused than ever. He knew his father, who had worked his way up in the world, believed that anyone who was determined could make something of him or herself. And Todd had always admired his father, both for his success and for his generosity. But this was going too far. Mr. Wilkins was actually encouraging Todd to befriend the person whom Todd had helped to send to prison!

Mr. Wilkins obviously believed what he'd heard from his Varitronics colleague. But what if Ned Rolleri was unknowingly passing along false information? Of course the Holmes family would want people to think Kevin had reformed. From what he knew about Mr. Holmes, Todd guessed he'd been glad to ship Kevin out of town and remove the tarnish from the family name. As he pictured the ice-hard man who had offered him the bribe, Todd felt a twinge of pity for Harry Holmes's son.

"Have some more fettucine," Mrs. Wilkins urged.

Todd let his mother refill his plate even though he knew he wouldn't be able to eat it. His appetite was gone, along with his desire to share his concerns about Kevin. He'd have to handle Kevin on his own, without help from anyone.

It was only the second day of camp but Todd felt as if he'd been in this uncertain and uncomfortable situation for weeks. *Why is Kevin so relaxed,* he wondered as he watched Kevin show a small camper how to dribble a basketball, *and I'm so nervous? He's the one with a criminal record, not me!* But ever-present in Todd's mind was the troubling secret of Kevin's past and of their unsettling conversation four days earlier. What exactly had Kevin been getting at, telling Todd he knew all about his family and Elizabeth? How could he be so certain Todd wouldn't give him away? Kevin's vague statements were almost more disturbing than an explicit threat. Todd was kept off balance, left on the edge, asking himself questions for which there were no easy answers.

A bell rang, indicating that it was time for the campers to rotate activities. Elizabeth approached the sports area followed by two clusters of kids.

"You look like the Pied Piper," Todd told her with a grin.

She smiled. "I'll trade you some Otters and Pumas for your Coyotes and Chameleons."

"You've got a deal." As Todd spoke, he noticed that Elizabeth's gaze had shifted. He turned to discover Kevin was standing at his side.

"I think it's time for the Otters and Pumas to learn how to play volleyball," Kevin announced. "What do you say, Wilkins?"

What could he say? As usual, Kevin was so cheerful and enthusiastic, there was nothing to do but go along with his suggestions. Todd had been letting him take the lead all day. He shrugged. "Fine with me."

"How 'bout a quick huddle?" Kevin dashed off to collect Jessica. With his arm around her shoulders, he steered her toward Todd. When the three stood close together, Kevin kept his arm around Jessica. "I like this part," he said, winking at Todd.

Todd could see that Jessica liked it, too. But Kevin's attentions to Jessica made Todd even more uneasy.

"Let's start with a demonstration," Kevin suggested. "You and I will hit the ball back and forth for a few minutes to show the different kinds of shots, OK, Todd? Meanwhile, Jessica will make sure all the kids know the proper way to position their hands."

Jessica fluttered her eyelashes at Kevin. "Good plan."

Todd grunted his assent. Side by side, he and

Kevin strode onto the lawn where the volleyball net was set up.

Kevin grabbed a volleyball from a big cardboard box filled with sports equipment. He twirled the ball on his forefinger for a few seconds, then flashed Todd a challenging grin. "Ready, Wilkins?"

Todd took up his position on the other side of the net. "When you are," he responded.

"This is how it's done, kids," Kevin boomed, serving the ball to Todd.

Todd made an easy overhead return. "See how he kept his fingers slightly bent but still stiff?" Kevin called to the watching campers. "Don't let those fingers crumple!" Kevin returned Todd's shot underhand style. He continued the instruction. "Your hands should be tightly clasped on those low shots. Thumbs on top."

Kevin's ball went high. Todd returned it with a gentle spike. "Whoa, a power shot," Jessica observed from the sideline.

Todd glanced her way and saw that he and Kevin had an audience. Enid and Aaron had joined Elizabeth and the Coyotes and Chameleons lingering on their way to the nature trails in order to watch the volleyball demonstration. Winston, Melissa, Ed, and their group of campers were watching from the picnic tables outside the lodge where they were working on an arts-and-crafts project.

"The harder they hit it to you, the harder you can hit it back," Kevin said lightly.

Todd had tapped the ball, but Kevin returned it with strength, forcing Todd to run for it. Todd's return sent Kevin way back. Jumping high, Kevin made the shot. Todd dove forward and connected with the ball only inches from the ground. Kevin spiked it back; Todd lunged.

Afterward, Todd couldn't have said at exactly what point the casual demonstration turned into a battle to the death. All he knew was that Kevin returned each shot a little more aggressively than the last. Todd grew competitive in spite of himself. He wasn't about to let the ball hit the ground; he wasn't about to let Kevin show him up. Kevin, who didn't even seem to be trying. Kevin, whose fixed, cold smile never altered. . . .

Kevin hit the ball deep. Sweat streaming down his face, Todd backed up for the shot and just barely made it. With Todd off balance and a long way from the net, Kevin had a golden opportunity, and he didn't pass it up. He tapped the ball lightly, using just enough force to drop it over the net. Todd made his best effort, but missed.

There was a resounding cheer from the spectators. Kevin bowed in their direction. "OK, kids," he shouted. Todd couldn't believe it; Kevin wasn't even winded. "Now it's your turn. Come on out here."

Kevin got the campers started in a game. Mopping his forehead on the sleeve of his

T-shirt, Todd joined Elizabeth and the others on the sidelines.

"Are you going to make it, old chum?" asked Winston with elaborate concern.

"I hate to say it, Wilkins, but he really gave you the runaround," Aaron observed.

Elizabeth jumped to Todd's defense. "Todd had Kevin running, too."

Todd winced. "It was just supposed to be a demonstration. I don't know what he was trying to prove!"

"What *he* was trying to prove?" Winston guffawed. "He wasn't trying to prove anything. He's still cool as a cucumber. You're the one that's worn out!"

"Admit it, Wilkins," Aaron kidded Todd. "He was toying with you. He could have nailed you a lot sooner if he'd wanted."

Todd forced a smile. "Maybe, maybe not."

At that moment Kevin came up behind Todd and clapped him on the shoulder. "Way to put on a show for the kids, Wilkins."

Todd wondered if the effort he was making to maintain a light attitude showed. "Anytime."

"How 'bout now?" Kevin laughed when Todd's face fell. "Just kidding, buddy. Take a breather."

Todd gritted his teeth and bit back the hot words. Kevin strolled back to the game, twirling a volleyball on his finger.

"My first impression was right," Jessica whispered to Cara later that afternoon, when the campers and counselors had gathered outside the lodge for a snack. "Kevin Holmes is my destiny." Jessica was even more enamored of Kevin since the volleyball duel with Todd. She was convinced she'd never met a boy so handsome, so cool, so strong.

"No doubt about it, he's gorgeous," Cara agreed, selecting a plum from an enormous bowl of fruit.

Jessica grabbed a peach. "You should see him move. Poetry in motion."

"Stop drooling," Cara teased. "Mr. Poetry-in-Motion has his eye on you."

"He does?" Jessica was pleased. "Then that's my cue. Catch you later!"

Flipping her blond hair over one shoulder, Jessica strolled in Kevin's direction.

"Hey," he greeted her. "How's my partner?"

"One of your partners," Jessica reminded him.

Kevin put a muscular arm around her shoulder and gave her a squeeze. A chill of excitement shivered up Jessica's spine. "My favorite partner," he said in what Jessica thought was an unbelievably sexy voice. "Don't tell Wilkins!"

She laughed. "I'm sure he'd be jealous."

"So tell me, Jessica." Jessica looked into Kevin's magnetic eyes, ready to tell him absolutely anything. "How come Wilkins went for your sister instead of you?"

"Oh." Jessica wrinkled her nose. "Liz is the

perfect match for Todd. He would never be my type."

"No? What type is he?" asked Kevin.

"The Mr. Nice Guy type," Jessica replied. "You know, everybody's best friend, a real upstanding citizen." She faked a yawn.

Kevin laughed. "A real upstanding citizen," he repeated. "Yeah, I'd say that was the impression I got."

Jessica was puzzled. "But I thought you didn't know Todd in Vermont."

"I didn't," Kevin corrected himself quickly. "What I meant was, that's the impression I'm getting."

"Oh, sure." Jessica wasn't really interested in talking about Todd. She wanted to talk about herself or about Kevin or, better yet, about how perfect the two of them would be together. "It really is a coincidence you moved to Sweet Valley. I'm so glad you did," she added meaningfully.

Kevin took one of her hands and looked deep into Jessica's eyes. She felt her knees buckle slightly. "I think it's more than just a coincidence." His voice was intense. "I think it's fate. Do you believe in fate, Jessica?"

Jessica nodded, a rapt expression on her face. *Do I ever!*

The Secca Lake beach was crowded with campers drying off after the end-of-day swim. The Eagle cluster was mingling with the Sandpipers; Todd and Elizabeth stood guard, holding hands.

Elizabeth's fingers tightened around his. "You're tense," she said to him. "I can feel it. Is something wrong?"

Todd shrugged. "Camp counseling is more work than I thought it would be," he said evasively.

"You mean you don't like it?" she asked, surprised.

"No, I like it. It's just kind of . . . tiring. That's all."

"Maybe it wouldn't be if you didn't push yourself all the time as if you were going for an Olympic medal," Elizabeth suggested with a teasing smile.

Todd knew Elizabeth was referring to his competition with Kevin. He felt himself tense up again. So she wouldn't feel it, too, Todd dropped her hand, but he kept his eyes on hers. *Why not tell her?* he thought suddenly. He hadn't been able to bring himself to confide in his parents the other night; it would feel good if at least one person understood what was going on between him and Kevin.

"It's not really the way it looks," Todd began.

"What isn't the way it looks?"

As he contemplated an explanation, Todd studied Elizabeth's expectant face. Then he swallowed the words that had risen to his lips. No, it was better not to get her involved. If the extent of Kevin's revenge was going to be beating him at sports, Todd supposed he could take it with good grace. He'd keep the secret he and Kevin shared.

As it became clear that Todd wasn't going to explain what he meant by that, Elizabeth's eyes clouded with disappointment. She turned away from him abruptly. "Time to go home, Sandpipers," she called. "Don't forget your towels."

Todd herded the Eagles around to the other side of Secca Lodge to wait for their rides home. Elizabeth was soon joined by Enid and Jessica; Winston and Aaron were talking with Kyle and Jill. Todd was left to himself.

"I've got my eye on you," a voice said quietly.

Todd jumped. Once again Kevin had taken him by surprise.

"You and your girlfriend look like you're pretty close," Kevin continued. "You probably tell each other everything." When Todd didn't answer, Kevin's eyes hardened. "Well, there's one thing you'd better not tell her about, and I think you know what it is. You'll be sorry if you slip up, Wilkins. I'll make sure of that."

"How will you make sure?" Todd challenged.

"Let's see," Kevin drawled. "How would you like it if someone you care about"—he paused and glanced pointedly in Elizabeth's direction— "got hurt?" Kevin didn't wait for a reply. He strolled off, his hands in his pockets. Todd was too shocked to stop him.

Todd mustered all of his self-control and tried to act cheerful as he and Elizabeth walked to the BMW fifteen minutes later. As he opened the door, Elizabeth gasped. "Oh, no. Look what someone did!" She pointed to the broken passenger's window.

Todd bent to peer through the shattered glass. "They got the window on the other side, too," he observed grimly. "And the glove compartment is open though nothing seems to be missing."

"I don't understand how someone can destroy another person's property just for kicks," Elizabeth exclaimed.

Just for kicks. Todd didn't think this was a case of random vandalism. He had a feeling it was a message—from Kevin. Kevin was letting Todd know in no uncertain terms he'd make good on his threat to hurt somebody Todd cared about if he talked.

Kevin Holmes hadn't reformed. He was still disturbed, and dangerous. Todd's heart thumped as he looked at Elizabeth, the most precious person in his life. If he couldn't warn people about Kevin without endangering her, Todd knew that, at least for the time being, he'd have to keep Kevin's secret.

Five

On Wednesday morning Mr. Schiavitti announced that instead of breaking up into the usual activity groups, all campers and counselors would participate in an informal half day hike around the lake.

"I like this idea," Enid said to Elizabeth as they sat in the lodge lacing their hiking boots. "You and Aaron and I don't have to do our flora-and-fauna routine."

"We're not off-duty, though," Elizabeth reminded her. "We're still responsible for keeping an eye on our cluster."

"True." Enid sighed. "And the Grizzly cluster likes to head in eight different directions at once. 'Single file' is just not in their vocabulary!"

Elizabeth hoisted a backpack containing a

first-aid kit, a water bottle, and snacks for her cluster. The moment she stepped outside the lodge, Todd hurried to her side.

"I'm glad I caught you," Todd said, slightly out of breath. "I had to drop off my car at the garage to get the windows replaced."

"How long will it be in the shop?" Elizabeth asked, concerned.

"The mechanic said he'd probably be finished with it this afternoon." Todd put his arm protectively around Elizabeth. "Let's hike together," he suggested.

Elizabeth squinted against the hazy morning sun and smiled up at him. "Sure. But it's a package deal, you know. I'm going to have eight Sandpipers in tow!"

"That's OK." Todd took her hand and gripped it tightly. "I just want to be with you."

The unexpected emotion in Todd's voice made Elizabeth's face flood with warmth. Lately he had been so distant; she thought he'd forgotten that part of the reason they had volunteered to be camp counselors was to add some variety to their relationship, to rejuvenate their feelings for each other. She'd even begun to suspect that Todd regretted signing up for the job. So far, they'd refrained from kissing in front of the campers, but now Elizabeth couldn't hold back. Standing on tiptoe, she brushed his cheek with her lips. "I love you," she whispered.

He wrapped his arms around her in a quick, possessive hug. "I love you, too, Liz."

"Hey, none of that!" a cheerful voice commanded.

Elizabeth stepped back and laughed. Kevin shook his finger at her. "I could report you to the camp director," he threatened playfully. "For setting a dangerous example."

At that moment Jessica marched up, carrying her backpack by the straps. Kevin seized her and dipped her low in a dramatic embrace. Jessica squealed. The campers cheered. "See what you've started?" Kevin teased Elizabeth.

She looked up at Todd and shook her head. "What a nut, huh?"

Elizabeth expected Todd to be as entertained by Kevin's antics as she was. But Todd didn't crack a smile. "Umm," he grunted, his mouth frozen in a tight line.

Elizabeth felt as if a bucket of cold water had just been splashed in her face. In all the time she'd known Todd, she'd never considered him to be moody. But lately there was no other way to describe his behavior. A minute ago he'd been warm and open with her; now he was wearing a distant, preoccupied look again.

Well, I can't worry about it now, she decided. All her attention belonged to the Sandpiper cluster.

Winston and the Chameleon cluster, Jill and the Coyotes, Kyle's Mustangs, and Enid's Grizzlies had already started off into the woods. Elizabeth waved to the Sandpipers. "Let's go!"

Elizabeth and Todd fell into step behind the Grizzlies; Kevin's Otters and Jessica's Pumas were immediately behind them, with Aaron, Cara, Melissa, and Ed and their clusters bringing up the rear. Sheltered by a thick canopy of leaves, the nature trail was dim and cool.

Elizabeth walked at a relaxed pace, periodically counting heads to make sure she had her whole cluster in view. Todd stayed close by her side, so close in fact that at one point, when the trail narrowed, he almost knocked her off the path. "Todd!" Elizabeth exclaimed.

Todd grabbed her arm to steady her. "Sorry," he said sheepishly.

"I'm not a toddler, you know. I can walk pretty well on my own at this point!"

Todd glanced back over his shoulder. "I just want to be near you," he explained. "Anything wrong with that?"

"Of course not." Elizabeth turned and followed the direction of Todd's gaze. All she saw was Kevin and one of his campers reading a trail marker on a tree trunk.

They walked on in silence. Elizabeth was puzzled. Todd said he wanted to be close to her, but it was a strange kind of close. He didn't seem to be enjoying her company; he didn't want to talk or hold her hand. He was just *watching* her.

There was a shout of excitement from up

ahead. A few of Enid's campers had spotted a fox. The Eagle and Sandpiper clusters darted forward, all hoping for a view. Elizabeth stayed on their heels. She counted heads, but this time she came up one short. *Calvin Kimball*, she realized. *As usual!* Of all the Sandpipers, six-year-old Calvin was the hardest to keep track of. Every thirty seconds something new captivated his curiosity. Elizabeth rapidly scanned the surrounding woods and thought she glimpsed a flash of Calvin's tow-blond hair. *He's probably tracking the fox*, she guessed as she plunged into the undergrowth.

It only took Elizabeth a minute to catch up with Calvin. "Come on, Liz!" Calvin shouted. "Let's catch the fox. He went that way!"

"But *we're* going *this* way." Elizabeth picked him up and pointed him toward the trail. "We've talked about how important it is to stay with the cluster, haven't we?" she said, trying not to giggle at the comical expression on Calvin's freckled face.

"Yeah, but—"

"No buts. Next time you want to go exploring, let me know first, OK?"

Hand in hand, the two headed back to the trail. Suddenly, Kevin popped out from behind a tree. "I saw you sprint off," he explained to Elizabeth. "I thought you might need some help so I asked Jessica to watch my cluster for a minute."

"Thanks, Kevin. I think I've got the situation

under control." Elizabeth displayed Calvin's hand, gripped firmly in hers. "We're going to walk like this for the rest of the hike. Pretend we're handcuffed together," she instructed Calvin.

The three had taken only a few steps in the direction of the trail when they were startled by the crackle of branches breaking. All of a sudden, Todd burst through the trees, a wild look in his brown eyes.

"Liz!" he cried hoarsely. "Holmes, what are you—Liz, are you all right?"

"Of course I'm all right! Calvin wandered off, that's all. Kevin followed to see if I needed help. Jessica's watching the Otters for him. Who's watching the Eagles?"

Todd looked back toward the trail. "No one. But I thought—"

Elizabeth bit her lip to keep from snapping at Todd in front of Kevin and Calvin. Kevin appeared to be trying hard not to smile; Elizabeth thought he was amused by the way Calvin was squirming in her grasp.

As soon as they were back on the trail and Kevin had rejoined Jessica, Elizabeth released Calvin's hand. The little boy trotted off after the rest of his cluster and Elizabeth spun to face Todd. "For your information," she said in a low, taut voice, "I can take care of myself. You're supposed to be guarding the kids, not me!"

"I know." Todd's broad shoulders slumped. "But you disappeared and I—I thought . . ."

Elizabeth studied Todd's frowning profile. There was a long pause. "Something's bothering you, Todd," she said at last. "What is it?"

"Nothing. Nothing's bothering me."

Todd's overemphatic tone rang false to Elizabeth's ears. She knew he was lying. Her characteristic patience gave way to frustration. "Something's been wrong for days, and I'm getting tired of trying to read your mind. Is it me? Is it something I did or said?"

"No," Todd assured her. "It's nothing *you* said or did."

"It's this camp-counseling thing, then," Elizabeth guessed. "You're not enjoying yourself, that much is obvious. Maybe you would have been happier working at your father's office this summer!"

"Maybe I would have," Todd agreed quietly.

Elizabeth was stunned. Todd had as much as admitted he wished he'd never signed up to be a camp counselor with her. Maybe he didn't care about their goal of rekindling their romance. Things between them were getting worse instead of better.

Elizabeth and Todd trudged on in silence. Though Elizabeth kept her eyes on her cluster of campers, her thoughts were centered on the subject of her relationship with Todd. A premonition chilled Elizabeth's heart. *It's not going to work out for us.*

Elizabeth peeked at Todd out of the corner of her eye. At that moment, her boyfriend might as well have been a stranger; she felt as if she didn't know him at all. When had this happened? *How* had it happened?

Todd was relieved when the hikers returned to the lodge on the east side of the lake. As the kids jostled for places in line by the grills, Todd threw himself down on the grass in the shade and closed his eyes.

Way to make a total fool of yourself, Wilkins. Todd pictured the scene in the woods an hour earlier. Elizabeth had been baffled by his behavior; Kevin had been amused. Todd opened his eyes and inspected the scratches on his legs. He must have looked like an idiot, barreling through the bushes. Who could blame Holmes for getting a kick out of the performance? But Todd hadn't been able to help himself. He shivered, recalling the moment he discovered that Kevin as well as Elizabeth had disappeared into the woods. Kevin's threat to harm someone Todd loved had echoed in his ears as he raced after Elizabeth. But everything had been fine. Ostensibly, Kevin's intention had been to help Elizabeth, not hurt her. This time, anyway.

The afternoon would be better, Todd told himself. The counselors would be back in their ordinary groups, which meant Elizabeth would be safe with Enid and Aaron while Todd would have a chance to keep an eye on Kevin. Not that he wanted to keep an eye on Kevin. Part of the reason for his anxiety was that Kevin seemed to be everywhere he turned. Todd wasn't allowed to forget Kevin or his chilling threats for one minute. But as much as Kevin's presence disturbed him, Kevin's absence worried him a lot more.

After lunch the Coyote, Puma, and Sandpiper clusters played sports. For an hour, Todd managed to keep a volleyball game going and simultaneously to spy on Kevin, who was coaching basketball. At one point Todd's heart almost stopped. Kevin was off to the side of the basketball court, standing very close to a slim, blond girl.

Jessica, Todd realized. He relaxed his hands, which he'd clenched into fists. His palms were sweating. It was only Jessica. Not that Todd was happy seeing Jessica with Kevin. He suspected Kevin was paying attention to his girlfriend's sister largely to irritate Todd.

I've got to stop imagining that the worst is happening, Todd commanded himself. After all, he hadn't broken his silence about Kevin's criminal past. And maybe Kevin wouldn't really hurt Elizabeth even if Todd told.

I'm not going to find out because I'm not going to tell, Todd thought as he helped one of the campers with a volleyball serve. Why would he tell, anyway? What good would it do? Mr. Schiavitti and the counselors probably wouldn't believe him. They were all under the spell of Kevin's winning facade.

He wasn't going to tell, but he was going to stay alert. He wouldn't stop worrying about Kevin Holmes until camp was over in a week and a half. Would he stop even then? A terrible thought crossed Todd's mind. What if Kevin stayed on in Sweet Valley? Todd realized he didn't know anything about Kevin's plans. What was Kevin really after?

At the end of the hour, there was a five-minute break before the campers rotated to the next activity. Jessica passed out granola bars to the Sandpipers, Pumas, and Coyotes; Todd grabbed a basketball. He had so much nervous energy boiling inside him, he decided to shoot some baskets to release it.

Todd dribbled the ball close to the basket, then made a shot. *Swish.*

"Two points!"

The familiar voice made the hair on the back of Todd's neck stand up. He didn't turn; he wasn't in the mood for Kevin's eerie smile.

Todd shot again. This time he missed, and before he could grab the rebound, Kevin had taken the ball. Kevin dribbled around Todd, making it look as if Todd were trying to prevent him from shooting. Todd was forced into a defensive position; when Kevin went to shoot, Todd instinctively raised his arms to block him.

"You want to play a little one-on-one, huh?" Kevin said, neatly managing to attribute the idea to Todd. Then he dodged around Todd and made the basket.

Todd took possession of the ball on the rebound, but Kevin was quick on his feet. In order to get past Kevin to shoot, Todd was forced to perform some of his fanciest footwork. "Way to move, Whizzer Wilkins!" Todd heard Winston shout.

Todd saw that, once again, he and Kevin had an audience. Winston wasn't the only one watching—Elizabeth, Jessica, Aaron, Ed, Kyle, and a bunch of campers had gathered along the sideline, too. Todd felt manipulated. All he'd wanted to do was casually shoot a few baskets, and Kevin had turned it into a floor show.

Well, I'll shoot my baskets, Todd determined. *Kevin Holmes isn't going to stop me.*

Five minutes later, Todd was forced to recognize that Kevin *had* stopped him. In the fast and furious one-on-one contest that had ensued, Kevin had scored fourteen points while keeping Todd to only six.

When Todd tried for a fourth basket and missed, Kevin grabbed the ball and bounced it off to the side. "Time to cool off," he suggested cheerfully.

Breathing heavily, his dark hair damp with perspiration, Todd walked off the court. Aaron handed him a towel. "I'd say you're lucky, Wilkins."

"In what way?" Todd asked, mopping his forehead.

"Lucky that Holmes already graduated from high school. You could have a tough time holding onto your position if he were trying out for Sweet Valley High's basketball team in the fall!"

"I'd have to learn a new cheer," Jessica kidded. " 'Holmes, Holmes, he's our man—' "

"I was just getting warmed up," Todd said. "I would've turned the tables if we'd played a few minutes longer." Somehow the words didn't come out as lightly as Todd had meant them to. From his friends' reactions Todd realized he'd sounded as if he were making excuses, as if he were a sore loser.

Aaron raised his eyebrows, clearly surprised at Todd's bad attitude. "Yeah, sure." He slapped Todd on the shoulder and then turned away to talk to Kevin.

"Chill out, Wilkins," Winston advised kindly before also leaving Todd to join Kevin.

Jessica flounced off with a sniff.

As Aaron, Winston, and Jessica complimented Kevin on his athletic prowess, Todd squatted to relace one of his sneakers. He tuned in to a conversation taking place behind him.

"Holmes was just messing around, but Wilkins takes himself so seriously, you'd think he was trying out for the NBA or something," a boy said.

"He's incredibly aggressive," a girl's voice contributed.

"He wanted to get into something with Holmes," said a second boy. "Serves him right that Holmes whipped him!"

Todd didn't look over his shoulder, but he

was pretty sure he knew who was speaking: Melissa and Ed from Fort Carroll and Kyle from Big Mesa. And he couldn't really blame them for their impression of him as aggressive and maybe even mean. Todd hadn't been himself since camp started and he knew it.

He wished he could turn around and tell them he wasn't really like that. *"It's Kevin. He's the bad guy,"* he wanted to say. But that wasn't an option. Todd knew he would come across as even more of a poor sport if he tried to defend his behavior.

Todd stood up and glanced over at the animated group surrounding Kevin. Across the top of Jessica's bright blond head, Kevin met Todd's eyes and grinned. Todd knew that to anyone else it would look like a friendly, "Hey, no hard feelings, right?" type of smile; for Todd, however, the smile had an edge as sharp as a razor. Kevin wasn't just triumphant because he'd beaten Todd at hoops. *He's beating me at some other game*, Todd thought. But he didn't know the name of that game, and Kevin was making up the rules as they went along.

Todd squared his shoulders, swallowed his pride, and kept quiet.

When the kids went home at four-thirty that afternoon, the counselors headed straight to the Dairi Burger. For a moment in the parking lot at Secca Lake, Todd had hesitated, and Elizabeth thought that once again he was going to opt out of socializing with the other counselors. She offered to drop him at the garage on her way to the Dairi Burger so he could pick up his car. Maybe he'd anticipated her disappointment; maybe he was trying to make up to her for their spat during the hike that morning. Whatever the reason, Todd had decided to join the others.

Now Elizabeth, Todd, Jessica, Kevin, Aaron, and Dana, who had met them at the Dairi Burger after rehearsal, were squished in a booth, devouring double cheeseburgers and French fries. "I have never been so hungry in my whole life," Jessica declared.

"It's from spending all day in the great outdoors," Aaron said.

Kevin grinned across the booth at Todd. "We sports counselors are getting a lot of exercise, eh, Wilkins?"

Elizabeth observed their interchange. Kevin's smile was friendly; he wasn't making a dig. But Todd seemed to have a hard time returning Kevin's smile. Elizabeth told herself that Todd was just tired and hungry. He couldn't really be holding a grudge against Kevin for something as silly as losing a one-on-one basketball game! She hadn't witnessed the duel herself, but according to Jessica, Todd had bullied Kevin into competing, then sulked when Kevin outscored him. It didn't sound like her boyfriend's character, but it was as obvious to Elizabeth as it was to everyone else that Todd was developing an animosity toward Kevin.

Kevin had finished his French fries and now he helped himself to one of Jessica's. "I'm helping you eat those," he informed her, "because I don't want you to spoil your appetite. I was hoping you'd have dinner with me later."

Jessica and Kevin had been spending a lot of time together at camp, but Elizabeth knew Jessica was hoping for something more than just a friendship. Elizabeth was impressed by her twin's self-control. "I'd like that," Jessica said casually.

"I'm counting on you to show me some of the fun spots in Sweet Valley," Kevin told her. "I'm still learning my way around."

Elizabeth leaned forward and put her elbows on the table. She realized she didn't know much about Kevin's life beyond the fact that he was living alone in a rented apartment downtown. "What have you seen and done around here so far?"

"Before camp started, I spent a lot of time at the beach. Reading, thinking . . . planning," Kevin responded. "I drove up and down the coast sightseeing."

"And you fell in love with southern California," Jessica concluded hopefully. "You're going to stay forever and never go back to Vermont!"

Kevin chuckled. "It's true, this is a beautiful part of the country. There's a lot to tempt me to stick around."

"But your parents probably want you to move back to Vermont at some point, maybe for college?" Elizabeth guessed.

"My parents . . . yeah, they'd like me to move back—eventually. When I've accomplished what I came out here for." Kevin's eyes shifted to Todd.

Elizabeth felt Todd's body tense. "Which is?" Todd prompted, his tone oddly serious.

Kevin laughed heartily. "What's that corny expression? 'Find yourself'—something like that. I'm finding myself."

"I give you a lot of credit," Dana said. "Going off on your own. That takes guts."

"Maybe." Kevin shrugged modestly. "But as I was saying to Jessica the other day, fate's got a hand in it, too. You can get something started, but who really knows where it's going to end?"

Todd jerked his arm and knocked over his soda. For a moment they were all distracted, piling paper napkins on the spill. Then Elizabeth returned to the subject of Jessica and Kevin's dinner date. "You know where you two should go?" she said. "Tiberino's. It has the best Italian food in town."

"Sounds great," Kevin said enthusiastically. "You know . . ." He looked from Elizabeth to

Todd and back again. "Why don't you guys come, too? We could make it a foursome."

Kevin's idea sounded like fun to Elizabeth; it had been a while since she and Jessica had double-dated. And maybe, she thought, an evening together would help ease the friction between Todd and Kevin. But it was up to Jessica; Elizabeth didn't want to intrude where she wasn't wanted. She caught her twin's eye.

Jessica nodded. "How about dinner and then dancing?"

Kevin turned to Todd. "What do you say, Wilkins?"

Todd hesitated, then said slowly, "Sure. It's OK with me."

"You know," Kevin began in a confiding tone, "it's been great getting to know everyone. It really wasn't that easy, moving someplace entirely new and not knowing a soul. But what a coincidence, huh? Bumping into someone from home, I mean." Kevin flashed Todd a bright smile. "The last time I talked to my dad, I mentioned your name and he suggested I ask your father for advice about job opportunities in Sweet Valley."

"Well, I know what we could do." Jessica looked at Todd. "How about meeting at your house before we go out? That way, Kevin would have a chance to meet your dad."

Kevin seemed pleased with this idea, and Jessica seemed pleased that *he* was pleased. "I'd love to meet your parents," Kevin told Todd sincerely.

"Well, uh . . ." Todd mumbled. For a moment Elizabeth thought her boyfriend was going to veto the plan. Finally, however, he shrugged once again. "All right. Fine," Todd assented, his tone as flat as the expression on his face.

Six

By that evening Todd had psyched himself up to pretend to be in an upbeat mood. He'd been caught off guard again at the Dairi Burger. He was sure his reluctance to double with Kevin and Jessica, and particularly to have everybody over to his house first, had been obvious.

Maybe Liz didn't notice, Todd thought hopefully as he slipped a clean polo shirt over his head. Kevin had noticed, though, and had clearly enjoyed Todd's discomfort. Well, Kevin wasn't going to see him sweat tonight. If Kevin was going to continue to put Todd in awkward situations, Todd would just have to stay one step ahead of the game. Kevin had the advantage; he'd threatened retaliation if Todd revealed his criminal past. But that didn't mean a showdown was inevitable. *I just have to steer clear of him, not let him manipulate me.*

Todd ran a comb through his damp hair and frowned at his reflection in the mirror. It wasn't going to be easy, though, with Kevin insinuating himself into Todd's life and continually inviting confrontation. And what if these two weeks were just the beginning? Todd tried to imagine a whole summer, a year maybe, of Kevin's cat-and-mouse games. The suspense of it all was completely unnerving. Todd couldn't figure Kevin out. He had no idea what Kevin would do next.

Mrs. Wilkins had set a pitcher of iced tea and a tray of hors d'oeuvres on the patio table. Together Todd and his father sampled the vegetable dip. "Pretty good," Todd commented as he reached for another carrot stick.

"I'm glad you invited Kevin over," Mr. Wilkins remarked as he dipped a broccoli floret. "I'm glad you two boys have made peace."

Todd didn't tell his father that, on the contrary, he and Kevin had started a new kind of war. "Liz and Jessica really like Kevin," he said instead. "All the kids at camp do. By the way, I never told anyone about what happened in Vermont, not even Liz. So maybe you should act as if you're meeting him for the first time."

"We are, in a way," said Mrs. Wilkins. "It sounds as if he really is a new boy."

Mr. Wilkins clapped a hand on Todd's shoulder. "You did the right thing, giving Kevin a chance to be judged by how he conducts himself in the present, instead of by how he handled himself in the past. I'm proud of your behavior, son."

Todd snapped a celery stick in two. He wasn't so sure his behavior was praiseworthy. At that moment he was once more tempted to tell his parents about what had transpired between him and Kevin during the last few days.

Before Todd had a chance to speak, the doorbell rang. Kevin, Elizabeth, and Jessica had driven over together in Kevin's Mazda. Todd ushered them through the house to the patio, feeling a bit like the odd man out. Elizabeth and Jessica were still laughing at some story of Kevin's. "I'm sorry," Elizabeth said at last, wiping her eyes. "But every time I picture you barreling down that hill on one ski with no poles—"

She and Jessica burst into giggles again. Kevin grinned at Todd. "I was just telling them what a fine figure I cut back in Vermont."

On the surface, Kevin's remark was completely natural and innocent. For Todd, however, it had a hidden and unpleasant significance. Todd's jaw tightened. Kevin's smile widened. *Liz and Jessica are laughing with Kevin*, Todd realized with irritation, *and Kevin's laughing at me*.

They reached the patio. As the twins greeted Todd's parents, something occurred to Todd. Kevin had never actually been introduced to Mr. and Mrs. Wilkins, though he'd seen them at the trial. This encounter had to be somewhat awkward for Kevin. Would he finally lose some of his composure? Todd cleared his throat. "Mom and Dad, this is Kevin Holmes from Vermont."

Kevin shook Mrs. Wilkins' hand first. "Thank you for having me over," he said politely. "You have a beautiful home." He turned to Mr. Wilkins. "I'm glad to meet you, sir. I've heard a lot about you from my father. It sounds as if you're missed by the Burlington business community."

"I wish I could have spent more time in Vermont," Mr. Wilkins replied. "But Varitronics had another plan."

"Varitronics is an impressive operation." Kevin accepted a glass of iced tea from Mrs. Wilkins. "I heard that the Burlington office doubled in size since it opened a couple of years ago. Are you seeing that sort of growth throughout the country?"

Todd nearly choked on his carrot stick. Kevin couldn't be serious!

Jessica could tell that this conversation wasn't going to interest her. "Didn't Liz tell me you're thinking of re-landscaping the pool area, Mrs. Wilkins?"

Mrs. Wilkins and Jessica wandered off toward the swimming pool. Mr. Wilkins, meanwhile, was clearly delighted by Kevin's interest in Varitronics. "The Northeast is an up-and-coming market for us," he replied. "We're not seeing quite the same gains in every region. On the whole, though, Varitronics is more competitive than ever."

"Information systems is a cutthroat field," Kevin observed. "It seems like every day some company is making a new product announcement."

"You must keep up with the business section of the newspaper," Mr. Wilkins said with a wink at Todd.

Todd smiled weakly. His father was always ribbing him for turning right to the sports pages.

Kevin nodded. "My dad thinks everybody should be required by law to read *The Wall Street Journal* with their breakfast."

Mr. Wilkins chuckled. "So tell me, Kevin," he continued. "What brought you to Sweet Valley? What are your plans for the future?"

"What are your plans for the future"—Dad's favorite question, Todd thought grimly.

But Kevin had no trouble fielding it. "I came to California to be on my own for a while. I'd like to work for a year or two before I go to college. I want to make sure I know what I'm after so I use my education to the best advantage. As soon as this day camp is over, I'll be looking for a job."

"Tell you what." Mr. Wilkins leaned back in his deck chair. "Why don't you stop by Varitronics some day next week? I'll show you around the place. Maybe we can find a position for you, for the summer at least."

Todd's jaw tightened. Talk about fast work! In five minutes Kevin had managed to butter up Mr. Wilkins to the point at which he was practically offering him a job!

For a brief instant Kevin's eyes met Todd's. The gleam of triumph was unmistakable. "I don't have much experience," he said modestly, "although I hope someday to help my father with the family business."

"That's a fine ambition," Mr. Wilkins declared. "And I'm sure you'll take to the business world like a fish to water. It runs in the blood." He turned to Todd with a fond expression. "Which is why I'm still hoping to convince Todd to work at Varitronics this summer. I know once he gets involved, he'll be hooked on the challenge and excitement."

Mr. Wilkins, Kevin, and Elizabeth looked at Todd. He remained stubbornly silent. He could tell by Elizabeth's expression that she thought he was sulking because of his father's attention to Kevin. *And maybe I am*, Todd thought.

Todd made an effort to transform the lines of his face into a smile. "Interning at Varitronics would be a great experience, Dad," he said with false enthusiasm. "Don't count me out yet."

Mr. Wilkins beamed. "I certainly won't, son."

Elizabeth looked baffled by Todd's sudden

change of attitude. She pushed back her chair. "I'll be right back. I'm going to make sure Jessica isn't talking Mrs. Wilkins into making the summerhouse a disco!"

Kevin stood up as well. "I'll walk with you. I'd like to see the grounds." He held out his hand to Mr. Wilkins. "I'm looking forward to talking more about Varitronics, sir," he said earnestly.

"Me, too," said Mr. Wilkins. "I hope you'll consider this a home away from home and stop by often."

Kevin smiled blandly at Todd. "Thanks. I really appreciate your hospitality. It's a lot easier to start over when you've got friends."

Todd and Mr. Wilkins watched Elizabeth and Kevin stroll across the lawn in the direction of the summerhouse. Todd could see that Kevin's reference, both humble and subtle, to the past had touched and impressed his father. Todd had to hand it to Kevin. He'd navigated through a tough situation with grace and tact.

"What a fine young man," Mr. Wilkins remarked, smiling benevolently. "I was right about him, wasn't I? He's turned over a new leaf. It's a wonderful thing to see."

Todd didn't argue. Anything negative he said about Kevin would seem ungenerous and spiteful after Kevin's performance for Mr. Wilkins's benefit. And Kevin's threat continued to loom over Todd. Watching Kevin walking with Elizabeth, Todd couldn't possibly forget it.

"It would really be something for both you boys to be working at Varitronics," Mr. Wilkins said.

So much for staying one step ahead of Kevin, Todd thought hopelessly. The night wasn't getting off to a very good start.

What a perfect night! Jessica thought as the music slowed and she melted into Kevin's strong arms. Dancing under the stars with Kevin Holmes was pure heaven.

Earlier, at the Wilkinses' house, she'd started to regret the double-date idea when somebody, probably Todd, brought up the boring topic of Varitronics. They hadn't stayed long at the Wilkinses', though, and dinner at Tiberino's had more than made up for any boredom Jessica had endured. Now, resting her head on Kevin's shoulder, Jessica sighed happily. All through the meal, Kevin had told the funniest stories. Todd had hardly opened his mouth. By the time they ordered dessert, Jessica had once again decided in favor of double-dating. Todd was a perfect foil for Kevin. Kevin was smarter, better-looking, more fun, and a better athlete. *And he's mine*, Jessica thought, tipping her face to Kevin's so he could kiss her.

"This is a beautiful spot," Kevin murmured into her ear.

"Isn't it?" The Beach Disco played the best dance music in town, and a Sweet Valley High crowd was there almost every weekend, and on weeknights as well throughout the summer. "I come here a lot."

"You're a great dancer," Kevin complimented her. "I definitely like the California style."

The beat had picked up again and they danced apart. Jessica knew she looked her best in a black tank top and the pink suede miniskirt Lila had talked her into buying at Lisette's. "You mean they don't dance like this in Vermont?"

Kevin shook his head. "You know, I'm kind of tempted to try an experiment."

Jessica liked the sound of that. She lowered her lashes seductively. "Oh? What kind of experiment?"

"I'm curious to know whether your twin sister dances as well as you do," Kevin replied. "I might just have to cut in on her and Wilkins."

Jessica laughed. "If you want to find out for yourself, go ahead, but you can take my word for it. We're not identical in *every* way."

"I thought twins had some kind of special bond," Kevin said.

"Sure, but in general we have a standard sibling-type relationship. In other words, half the time we get along and half the time we drive each other crazy! How about you—do you have any sisters or brothers?"

"One brother," Kevin said after a pause. "An older brother. We weren't—aren't—much alike."

"Too bad for him," Jessica said lightly. Of

course Kevin's brother wasn't as wonderful as Kevin. Jessica was sure no one was.

Kevin laughed, but his eyes stayed cool. "Yeah, too bad for him."

Talking about other people's families bored Jessica. Unless the families were rich, that is. She'd liked what she'd learned about Mr. Holmes so far, and was eager to hear more. "I know your father owns his own company, but what kind of company is it?" she asked.

"The biggest R and D—that's research and development—firm in Vermont," Kevin answered.

"R and D. That must be very interesting," Jessica lied. It was only interesting, of course, if it was a good way to make a lot of money. "Will you and your brother join the company when you get out of college?"

"I'd like to."

They moved close again for another slow dance. Jessica didn't notice that Kevin's response had been somewhat evasive and that the expression in his eyes had gone from cool to hard. She was lost in a reverie about her future with Kevin. As soon as he took over the firm, she'd talk him into moving it from Burlington to Sweet Valley. . . .

Todd was sure he'd never suffered through such a long evening in his entire life. He'd been thrown off balance from the start by the way

Kevin won over his father in all of five minutes. Then, at Tiberino's, Todd had been rendered speechless by Kevin's stories about life in Vermont. Todd knew they were all lies, but Elizabeth and Jessica ate them up. There had been no point in contradicting Kevin at the restaurant, though. At some point—maybe soon—he might be forced to confront Kevin, but he would do it in private.

In the meantime, however, Todd felt humiliated by Kevin's constant manipulations. Kevin said and did things to disconcert him, then reveled in Todd's anxiety and confusion. Todd kept wondering: *What kind of revenge is he after?*

Todd had never felt less like dancing, but he forced himself to try. At least by dancing, he could stay close to Elizabeth and, by careful maneuvering, keep the two of them some distance from Jessica and Kevin.

Todd checked his watch. They'd been at the Beach Disco for an hour. In another hour he could suggest leaving.

At that moment someone tapped Todd on the shoulder. "May I?"

Todd turned and found himself staring into Kevin's pale, ironic eyes. Todd had no choice. Clenching his teeth, he stepped aside.

Kevin and Elizabeth moved off. Todd left the dance floor, but kept his eyes glued to Kevin and Elizabeth. *He's tormenting me*, Todd thought bitterly. Suddenly he was able to see some consistency in Kevin's behavior: the way Kevin was making Todd look bad at camp, the conversation with Mr. Wilkins about Varitronics that evening, and now dancing with Elizabeth. *He knows just what to do to get to me, and he's doing it.*

The song seemed to drone on forever; with every note Todd felt his heart pound harder. At last the song ended. But before Todd could make his way onto the dance floor to reclaim Elizabeth, another song had begun.

Todd saw Kevin put his arms around Elizabeth. Kevin said something and she laughed. It was maddening. Todd wanted to shout out the truth, that Kevin wasn't the fun, kind person everyone thought he was. Todd remembered Kevin's face the night of the brutal robbery in Vermont, Kevin's expression as he threatened Todd, and the shattered windows of the BMW. "How would you like it if someone you care about," Kevin had asked Todd, the bland smile never leaving his face, "got hurt?"

Todd couldn't remain inactive for a second longer. It was bad enough watching Kevin flirt with Jessica every day at the camp. But the anxiety Todd felt on Jessica's behalf was nothing compared to his outright fear for Elizabeth's safety. It was Elizabeth, not Jessica, whom Kevin had implied he would harm.

Todd bolted onto the dance floor and shoved his way through the swaying couples. He pushed Kevin aside unceremoniously. "Jessica's looking for you," he said.

Kevin stepped back, an amiable grin on his face. "Thanks for the dance, Liz."

Elizabeth stared at Todd in disbelief. As soon as Kevin was out of earshot, she exclaimed, "How could you be so rude?"

Todd knew he was guilty as charged. "I just didn't want you dancing with him anymore," he explained lamely. "I . . . I wanted to dance with you myself."

Elizabeth put her hands on her hips. "I can dance with whomever I want! What's the matter, don't you trust me?"

I trust you! Todd wanted to shout. *It's Kevin I don't trust.* He licked his lips. Maybe he couldn't tell Elizabeth the whole truth, but he owed her some explanation for his odd behavior. "There's just something I don't like about Kevin," he said.

Todd wasn't surprised that Elizabeth looked doubtful. What was not to like about fun-loving, good-natured Kevin Holmes? "What exactly is it about Kevin?"

"I can't put my finger on it," Todd answered vaguely.

Elizabeth shook her head. "I don't believe you, Todd Wilkins! Is this all sour grapes because of what's been going on at camp and because your father might find Kevin a job? When did you get so ridiculously, pointlessly competitive?"

"It's not sour grapes," he promised her. "It's not competition." But he couldn't say more than that. He couldn't defend himself. He couldn't reveal what he knew about Kevin and why he was being so overprotective. Not yet, anyway, not until he knew what Kevin was after. Given Kevin's potential for violence, Todd had to be sure he knew Kevin's plan before he attempted to counter it.

Wordlessly, Todd wrapped his arms firmly around Elizabeth. An embrace was no substitute for an honest answer, but for now it would have to do.

Seven

"Did you have fun last night?" Mrs. Wilkins asked Todd on Thursday morning.

Todd stood next to his mother at the kitchen counter and watched as she sliced a cantaloupe. He didn't want to start the day off with a lie. At the same time, if he admitted he'd had a terrible time the night before with Elizabeth, Kevin, and Jessica, he'd also have to explain why.

She'd listen. She always listens. His mom would be surprised and worried and sad to hear that Kevin hadn't reformed after all, to hear about his threats, but she would accept Todd's words and support him.

Suddenly Todd felt incredibly foolish for not having confided in her sooner. "Actually, Mom—"

"Good morning, family," Mr. Wilkins boomed cheerfully as he strode into the kitchen. "Fresh melon. My favorite. How was the Beach Disco, son?"

Todd sat down at the table with a slice of melon. "The Beach Disco was fine," he answered guardedly.

Mrs. Wilkins placed a carton of milk and three bowls of granola on the table. "It's really remarkable," she said. "Kevin must have had serious troubles of some sort in Vermont, but he's clearly in command of himself now."

Todd couldn't argue with that. *Kevin is in command of himself, and in command of me,* he thought as he poured milk on his cereal.

"It's important for the boy to make friends," Mr. Wilkins observed. "It's not an easy thing he's doing. He needs all the support he can get."

Todd looked at his father, tongue-tied by the irony. *I'm the one who needs your support.*

"I'm glad to see you making an effort to help him feel at home here, son," Mr. Wilkins continued. "Keep it up. Ask him over again soon. In fact, how about dinner tonight?" Mr. Wilkins looked at his wife, who smiled her agreement.

Todd swallowed. How had it come around to this? A minute earlier he'd been ready to share his concerns about Kevin with his mother; now such a conversation seemed impossible. It was almost as if his father's confidence in Kevin's turnaround invalidated Todd's own assurance of Kevin's bad nature.

Todd had to try, though. He cleared his throat. "I don't know about dinner, Dad," he said. "I don't really have the time, and, well . . . I'm just not sure I like Kevin all that much."

Mr. Wilkins frowned. "I know it's not easy, son, but you should make your best effort to get beyond what transpired between you and Kevin in Burlington."

Todd's shoulders slumped. That wasn't it at all. His father had it all wrong. Todd would have been willing to let bygones be bygones; it was Kevin who was keeping the past alive by pursuing his revenge.

Todd met his mother's eyes. Her expression was sympathetic, but Todd knew she was on his father's side. *Because she doesn't know my side.*

"I'll ask Kevin over, Dad," Todd said finally.

Mr. Wilkins beamed. "That's the spirit, Todd. We'll have a fine time."

Todd spooned into his granola. He doubted that very much.

"It's really nice of you to invite me over to your house," Kevin said to Todd with a sly smile.

Todd had stopped Kevin in the Secca Lake

95

parking lot after camp. He'd put off asking Kevin all day, hoping Kevin would have other plans.

"It wasn't exactly my idea," Todd replied stiffly. Being with Kevin all day at camp was bad enough; the thought of bringing him home afterward was almost intolerable. Todd felt a flash of resentment as he recalled his father virtually commanding him to invite Kevin for dinner. Then he recalled his own failure to explain the reason for his protest. He had no one but himself to blame for his predicament.

"I didn't think it was your idea." Kevin's eyes glinted with sadistic pleasure. "We'll have fun, though. We're going to be buddies, right?"

Before he realized what he was saying, Todd spoke the thought that had been on his mind for days. "What do you want from me, Holmes?"

"I don't want anything from you," Kevin replied. "Don't you feel, though, that our lives are somehow connected?"

"No," Todd said firmly. "No. We had a random encounter, one I'd rather forget."

"A random encounter," Kevin repeated. He laughed bitterly. "That's what it was to you. A random encounter you'd rather forget. Well, let me tell you something, Wilkins." Kevin's voice became harsh and menacing, but his composure remained intact. "I haven't forgotten it, and I won't ever forget it. We're connected, you and me, whether you like it or not." The shadow lifted from Kevin's eyes and once more he smiled. "See you later!"

Kevin sauntered off in the direction of his car. As Todd turned to head for the BMW, he realized that every muscle in his body was tense. He took a deep breath and willed himself to relax. He hated the way Kevin had the power to throw him off balance while never losing his own self-possession.

Todd examined the BMW's new windows which were indistinguishable from the original ones. He couldn't prove Kevin destroyed his property, but he was convinced nonetheless. Todd shuddered. It was those eyes, those pale green eyes that didn't give anything away. *Maybe there isn't anything to give away,* Todd thought as he started the car's engine. Maybe there was nothing behind them. Maybe Kevin Holmes didn't have a soul.

Todd had plenty of opportunity to look into Kevin's unreadable eyes at the dinner table that night. The meal was as unbearable as Todd had expected it would be, precisely because on the surface it was so pleasant. Kevin was slick and charming, complimenting Mrs. Wilkins on her cooking and continuing to demonstrate enthusiastic, respectful interest in Varitronics. Todd knew he was the only person at the table who was uncomfortable. And Todd knew Kevin knew.

"I think we have a match here," Mr. Wilkins said with obvious satisfaction. "You and Varitronics, Kevin."

"Do you think so?" Kevin asked.

"We're looking for sharp minds, young people hungry to be in on the action," Mr. Wilkins declared. "You have natural business sense, I can tell. You could learn a lot at Varitronics, and Varitronics would benefit as well. You must come by the office, Kevin, and get a feel for the whole scene."

I should be relieved Dad's grilling someone else for a change, Todd thought, moving the rice pilaf around on his plate with his fork. But he wasn't relieved in the least. He hated to see his kind-hearted father fooled by Kevin's charade. *Dad doesn't know Kevin's a con artist*, Todd reminded himself. *And he won't know—unless I tell him.*

"How about having dessert out on the patio?" Mrs. Wilkins suggested after Kevin had helped her clear the dinner plates. "It's a lovely evening."

"Sounds great, Mom," Todd said, trying to snap himself out of his preoccupation.

"May I help you bring it out?" Kevin offered.

"No, thank you," Mrs. Wilkins said. "You go on outside."

Todd wished he could excuse himself for the rest of the evening. He hoped Kevin would eat dessert quickly and leave. As Mr. Wilkins and

Kevin started in the direction of the patio, Todd hung back. "I have to make a phone call," he lied. "I'll be out in a minute."

Kevin smiled and Todd knew the other boy saw right through his lie. *I don't care,* Todd thought as he headed toward the recreation room. He needed a few minutes to himself, away from Kevin's disturbing presence.

In the rec room, Todd flung himself on the sofa and stared at the blank face of the big-screen TV. He picked up the phone and started to dial Elizabeth's number, then Aaron's. Finally he stood up. He couldn't hide out for the rest of the evening. *If Kevin can put on a show, so can I,* Todd determined. And maybe later he'd finally find a way to talk to his father about what was really going on.

Todd headed back toward the patio. As he passed the door to his father's study, he glanced in. What he saw stopped him in his tracks. Kevin was in the study, opening the top drawer of Mr. Wilkins's desk!

Todd paused for only a second; then he hurried on before Kevin could catch a glimpse of him. Todd realized he'd found his opportunity. He'd caught Kevin in the act of snooping in his father's desk. It was evidence, hard and unambiguous. His father would have to acknowledge he'd been deluded and that Kevin's reformation was all an act.

"Dad," Todd said in a low, urgent voice when he'd joined his father on the patio, "Kevin's in your study, going through your desk! It's proof, Dad. What you heard from your friend in Vermont was just a story. Kevin hasn't changed. I knew it already, Dad, because—"

Todd broke off. His father was glaring at him. "Todd, I'm astonished you could be so suspicious and unforgiving. I asked Kevin to bring me something from my desk. The Varitronics annual report."

The blood drained from Todd's face, then rushed back in a flush of embarrassment. "I— I didn't realize—"

Mr. Wilkins shook his head. "Refusing to forgive Kevin—being ready to accuse him on such slight grounds—is spiteful and childish. I expected better from you, Todd. I'm very disappointed."

Todd didn't know what to say in his own defense. His father was right about this particular incident. But he was still wrong about the rest of it. "I'm sorry," Todd said, for lack of a better response.

At that moment Todd saw Kevin standing at the French door that opened out onto the patio. He had returned from the study, annual report in hand, in time to overhear the tail end of the confrontation. As Kevin gave Todd a sly smile, Todd had to acknowledge he'd lost this round. Now there was no way Todd could tell his father about Kevin's threatening hold over him. Mr. Wilkins would assume Todd was being petty and vindictive. Mr. Wilkins was so charmed by Kevin, he wouldn't believe his own son.

This is like a bad dream, Todd thought. He looked on as his father and Kevin began to go over the Varitronics annual report. Kevin's expression was so earnest, his smile so genuine. Could this be the same devious, black-hearted person who had sworn he would hurt someone Todd loved if Todd revealed the secret of his past? What could cause someone with all of Kevin's economic advantages and personal gifts to go so wrong?

Todd had never felt so alone. A bond was being forged between Mr. Wilkins and Kevin; but between Todd and his father, the distance was growing.

I can't talk to my own father, Todd realized. He was on his own with this—with Kevin—with whatever Kevin was trying to do to him.

To commemerate the end of the first week of camp, a field day was being held Friday in place of the regular afternoon activities. After lunch, the campers and counselors gathered in front of Secca Lodge to hear Mr. Schiavitti explain how the afternoon games would be played.

"Counselors, you'll be pairing up," Mr. Schiavitti instructed, "so there will be two people to run each game."

Enid smiled at Elizabeth. "What do you say we take the watermelon-eating contest?"

"That one's mine," declared Winston, who'd come up behind them. "Although one of you young ladies may act as my assistant."

Enid rolled her eyes at Elizabeth. "You're too generous, Winston."

Winston grinned and reached for the back pocket of his khaki shorts. Then his smile turned into a frown. He patted his shorts anxiously. "My lucky baseball cap!" he exclaimed. "I could have sworn I put it in my pocket. Has anyone seen it?"

Elizabeth and Enid shook their heads. "Maybe it's in the lodge," Elizabeth suggested.

Winston ran inside to check. He reemerged a moment later looking gloomier than before. "No sign of it," he reported.

Just then they were joined by Kevin, his sandy hair still damp from the noontime swim. "No sign of what?" he asked.

"My lucky baseball cap," Winston said.

"You mean, the one you wear so often that I thought you'd had it surgically attached to your head?"

"That's the one. Have you seen it?"

"Not since before the swim," Kevin replied.

Winston sighed heavily. "It's just not going to be the same refereeing the watermelon-eating contest without my hat."

"It'll turn up," Enid assured him.

"The watermelon-eating contest," Mr. Schiavitti called out. "Who wants to take it?"

"We do!" Winston bellowed, holding up Enid's arm and his own.

Kevin smiled at Elizabeth. "Want to team up?"

"Sure!" Elizabeth agreed cheerfully. "Which event do you want to run?"

"I need two counselors for the wheelbarrow race," Mr. Schiavitti called out.

"Let's take it," Kevin said to Elizabeth.

At that instant Todd bounded across the grass to Elizabeth's side. He shouldered his way between Elizabeth and Kevin, and waved at the camp director. "Liz and I will run that one," he shouted.

"Todd!" Elizabeth burst out. She was mortified by his rudeness. It was like a rerun of the other night at the Beach Disco, when Todd had cut in on her and Kevin on the dance floor! "What are you—" Elizabeth bit back the rest of the question. She didn't want to make a scene in front of the entire camp.

"That's OK, Liz," Kevin said with an easy smile. "The tug-of-war is more my thing, anyway"

Elizabeth stomped out to the lawn where the games were being organized. She didn't look at Todd until they were well out of earshot of the campers and other counselors. Then she glared at him. "I can't believe you just did that!" she declared hotly. "What's gotten into you? Why do you keep acting like this?"

Todd avoided her gaze. "No particular reason."

"Don't give me that," Elizabeth snapped. "I know you and I know something's bugging you. And it's starting to bug me. Why are you being so overprotective?"

After a moment, Todd looked closely at Elizabeth. "It's Kevin."

"What *about* Kevin?" Elizabeth asked.

"I know he comes across like a pretty good guy," Todd said slowly. "But sometimes people aren't what they seem to be."

Elizabeth was frustrated by Todd's vague response. "What exactly are you saying?"

"Just that I'd like you to steer clear of Kevin. That's all."

Elizabeth frowned. "That's all?" she repeated. "For no particular reason, you're telling me not to be friends with Kevin, and then you say 'That's all'?"

"Liz . . ." Todd began. He put a hand on her arm and Elizabeth threw it off.

"Maybe you don't like Kevin," she said, "but I do." Suddenly Elizabeth had an uncomfortable insight. Did Todd dislike Kevin because Mr. Wilkins was being so nice to him, helping him find a job? Was Todd jealous? "Todd, why don't you like Kevin?"

Todd's jaw tightened, but he didn't answer

her question. Elizabeth could see the unhappiness in his eyes, but she didn't know what he was thinking. She couldn't read his mind. "It's not working, is it?" Elizabeth said after a long, strained silence. She struggled to keep her voice even; she could feel tears threatening. "Being at the camp together hasn't brought us any closer. If anything . . ." Elizabeth swallowed. It was going to be hard, but she knew what she had to say. She knew what she had to do if she wanted to save their relationship. "Maybe some time apart is what we need," she said at last. "To figure out whether our relationship is worth holding onto."

Her voice had dropped almost to a whisper. Todd stepped closer in order to hear her. He put his hands on her shoulders. "I want to hold on, Liz. I want to hold onto you. But I can't explain—"

Elizabeth twisted away from his touch. "You can't explain, but that means I can't understand you. And that's just not right. Until you can tell me what's on your mind, I don't think we should spend so much time together."

She waited for the import of her words to sink into Todd's mind. *Tell me I'm overreacting,* she prayed desperately. *Tell me where we've gone wrong. Tell me anything!*

Todd looked sadly at Elizabeth. It was as if a struggle of some kind were taking place inside him.

At last he spoke, but he didn't say the words she was hoping to hear. "If that's what you want."

Elizabeth nodded and turned away quickly so Todd wouldn't see the tears in her eyes.

Eight

"It was pretty wild," the twins' older brother, Steven, said to his family at dinner on Friday night. "We went out to the site and went head to head with the developers. I never thought law could be so exciting."

Mr. Wakefield grinned. "I guess corporate law seems pretty tame compared to environmental law."

"I'm not knocking what you do, Dad," Steven assured his father.

"I know you're not. And I had a feeling you'd like working for Delaney's firm this summer. Environmental law was a small field for a long time, but not anymore."

"I'm so glad you're enjoying yourself," Mrs. Wakefield said.

"I really am," said Steven. "We're already talking about a job for next summer, too."

As Elizabeth helped herself to salad, she thought how different this conversation was from those she'd witnessed between Todd and *his* parents. Elizabeth knew her father would be thrilled if Steven decided to go into law, but Mr. Wakefield never pushed the issue. He'd helped Steven find a summer job with a local law firm, but only after Steven had asked him for help. Mr. Wilkins, on the other hand, had left no room for doubt about which path in life he hoped, even expected, his only son would take.

No, Elizabeth thought as she speared a sun-dried tomato with her fork, the problem wasn't determining what Todd's father wanted. It was what *Todd* wanted that was a mystery.

Stop thinking about him! Elizabeth commanded herself. She didn't understand what was going on with Todd these days because he wouldn't give her a chance to understand. Elizabeth knew she'd done the right thing by insisting on some time apart so they could both think things through. *So why do I feel terrible?*

"The day camp is exciting, too," Jessica declared. "Isn't it, Liz?" She didn't wait for Elizabeth's confirmation. "We're meeting some fantastic people."

"So you really like working with children?" her mother asked.

"I'm not talking about *them*," Jessica said. "They don't count."

Elizabeth couldn't help but laugh. "What do you mean, they don't count? There are almost a hundred children!"

"Correct me if I'm wrong, but there wouldn't *be* a day camp if it weren't for the kids," Mr. Wakefield remarked.

"True." Jessica grinned, the dimple in her left cheek deepening. "The way I see it, though, the kids are a means to an end. Which reminds me." She pushed back her chair. "I'm meeting Lila and everybody else at the Beach Disco in an hour and I still have to take a shower. May I please be excused?"

Elizabeth stood up, too. She wasn't planning on going to the Beach Disco, but she was ready to spend some time alone with her thoughts.

As she trailed up the stairs after Jessica, Elizabeth sighed deeply. "I heard that," Jessica said, turning and looking inquiringly at her twin. "Are you still depressed about your necklace?"

Elizabeth put a hand to her throat. In her preoccupation with Todd, she'd almost forgotten about the missing necklace. She and Jessica wore matching gold lavalieres, sixteenth-birthday presents from their parents. After the field-day activities, there had been an all-camp swim in the lake. Before swimming, Elizabeth had removed her lavaliere and placed it with her other belongings in the lodge. Later, when she'd gone to put the necklace back on, she'd discovered it was missing.

She sighed again. "Oh, that. I'm sure it will

turn up. I'm just tired. I don't think I'm going to make it to the Beach Disco."

"But everybody's going to be there!" Jessica followed Elizabeth into her bedroom. "Aren't you meeting Todd?"

Elizabeth bit her lip to keep from bursting into tears and shook her head.

Jessica's forehead creased in a frown. "What's wrong, Liz? Did something happen between you and Todd?"

Elizabeth sank back against the pillows on her bed, pulled her knees up to her chest, and hugged them tightly. "Yeah."

Jessica sat down facing her sister. "Tell me," she ordered.

It was a relief for Elizabeth to tell her twin what had been happening with Todd. When she had finished relating their conversation of that afternoon, Jessica's eyes widened. "You mean, you broke *up*?"

Elizabeth shivered. It sounded so horrible, spoken out loud like that. "I guess we did. Temporarily, anyhow."

Jessica patted her sister's knee. "You guys have had little setbacks before," she reminded Elizabeth, her tone reassuring and practical. "You'll work things out. You always do."

Elizabeth usually appreciated Jessica's cheerleader-style pep talks. And Jessica was right; Elizabeth and Todd *had* gone through a lot together, and in the past they'd emerged from disagreements with their love and friendship stronger than ever. But Elizabeth's heart told her that this time was different.

"I'm not so sure," she told Jessica. "How can Todd and I work things out if we can't even talk to each other?"

Jessica wrinkled her nose. "You got me," she admitted. Then she bounced up from the bed. "But I do know you're not going to feel any better by sitting home tonight and moping. Come to the Beach Disco!"

Elizabeth shook her head. There was no way she wanted to dance; much less did she want to run into Todd. "I think I'll just curl up in bed with a book."

As soon as Jessica disappeared into the bathroom that connected the twins' bedrooms, Elizabeth rolled over and buried her face in a pillow. She had a feeling it was going to be a long, lonely weekend. *Maybe the longer the better*, she thought as one tear and then another rolled down her cheek. She wasn't looking forward to camp on Monday morning. Without Todd in her life, she wasn't looking forward to much of anything.

For days Todd had been looking forward to the weekend when he could finally escape from Kevin Holmes for a while. He'd imagined taking a day trip somewhere with Elizabeth, driving as far away from Sweet Valley as possible.

And now it was finally Saturday, but he and

Elizabeth had broken up. Todd had no idea where she was or what she was doing, no way of making sure she was safe. For all he knew, at that very moment she was hanging out with Kevin Holmes.

But Kevin won't hurt her, Todd reminded himself, *unless I give him a reason to.* And Todd wasn't planning to talk about Kevin, or about anything. Todd wasn't in the mood to see his friends. He'd be lying low.

Todd wandered into the rec room and found his father watching Saturday-afternoon sports on the big-screen TV. Todd hesitated in the doorway, reluctant to join him. Since the night Kevin had come over for dinner, Todd had been avoiding Mr. Wilkins. It wasn't hard to do; it was a big house.

Now Todd berated himself silently. *Don't be a coward and don't be a fool. It was a misunderstanding, that's all. Maybe he sided with Kevin, but he's still your father. Nothing will ever change that.*

"Hi, Dad," Todd said as he sat down next to Mr. Wilkins on the couch.

"How are you, son?" Mr. Wilkins responded somewhat coolly, his eyes still glued to the golf game on TV.

Todd took a deep breath. Just as he was about to speak the phone rang. Mr. Wilkins picked it up and said, "Hello." Todd watched as a smile creased his father's face. "Why, hello, Kevin! No, you're not catching me at a bad time. I'd be happy to answer a few more questions about Varitronics. Go ahead."

Quietly, Todd got to his feet and left the room.

Fifteen minutes later, he parked the BMW at the beach. He hadn't put on swim trunks; he just wanted to walk along the water's edge. Todd strolled north, away from the crowd of sunbathers and surfers, sandcastle builders and volleyball players. The salty breeze whipped his hair, and he squinted against the glare of the sun reflected off the white sand.

No man is an island, Todd thought, staring out over the ocean's endless expanse. *Who said that?* Well, it wasn't true. At that moment Todd felt very much like an island. He was more alone than he'd ever been in his entire life.

On Monday, Winston and Todd took a couple of the box lunches provided by the day camp and sprawled out on the grass under a tree. "I'm sorry things aren't going well for you and Liz."

Winston was staring at two people sitting on the other side of the lawn. Todd didn't want to look, but he couldn't help himself. It was Elizabeth—and Kevin. They were eating lunch together and talking animatedly. *It didn't take him long*, Todd thought grimly. Word had gotten around over the weekend that Todd and

Elizabeth had had a fight. True to her word, Elizabeth was keeping her distance from Todd, and the other camp counselors had picked up on the fact.

All morning Todd had been telling himself he was only imagining Kevin was paying more attention than usual to Elizabeth. Now the evidence was staring Todd right in the face. Kevin was pursuing Elizabeth. And Elizabeth didn't seem to mind.

"I thought Holmes was interested in Jessica," Winston mused.

Not trusting himself to speak, Todd shrugged and bit into his sandwich. The ham and cheese tasted like cardboard. Suddenly Todd was overwhelmed by the irony of the whole terrible situation. It was for Elizabeth's own safety, among other reasons, that he'd been keeping silent about Kevin. Now, as a result of his reticence, Todd had handed the one person he loved most over to his gravest enemy.

Winston crunched on an apple. "Don't worry, big guy," he said with forced cheerfulness. "You and Liz will be back together in no time. Kevin's no threat.'

Kevin's no threat. Todd almost laughed at Winston's innocent, well-intended words. *If only that were true!*

The day crawled by, and through every single minute of the day, Todd was conscious of the chilly, pained distance between him and Elizabeth. And Kevin never missed an opportunity to flirt with her. As campers and counselors gathered at the lake for the end-of-day swim, Todd saw he wasn't the only person who was annoyed by the sight of Kevin and Elizabeth's new rapport. A few yards down the beach, Jessica was standing with her hands on her hips, looking distinctly grumpy. "All right, Pumas, get in the water and swim," she snapped.

When all the campers went for a swim at the end of the day, each counselor guarded his or her own cluster. Todd waved his arm and the Eagles darted into the water, splashing and yelling. Taking advantage of his dark sunglasses, Todd shifted his gaze back and forth from the kids in the water to the spot further down the beach where Elizabeth and Kevin, whose clusters were swimming together, were standing. Kevin said something to Elizabeth that made her laugh, then put his arm around her. It was a casual gesture, but it cut Todd like a knife. *Don't touch her!* he wanted to shout.

All of a sudden Todd was jolted out of his distraction. Something was wrong in the water. Far out in the lake, there was splashing and panicked cries. A child was drowning!

Throwing his sunglasses on the sand, Todd sprinted into the water. Stroking for all he was worth, he swam straight for the little boy. The child's head was still above water. Red hair—was it Brian Daly, one of Todd's Eagles? *Hang in there*, Todd prayed.

He turned his head to suck in some air. As he did he saw he wasn't the only person rushing to the child's aid. A powerful swimmer came up beside Todd, passed him, and reached the drowning boy!

There were cheers from the shore as Kevin began swimming back, one arm supporting the distressed but uninjured child. For a moment Todd was stunned. He treaded water, breathing hard. Kevin. Of course, it had to be Kevin. Todd knew he shouldn't be surprised. When wasn't Kevin in the right place at the right time, the man of the moment?

Todd swam to shore, catching up with Kevin in time to help him carry Brian onto the beach. Elizabeth was ready with a towel. She wrapped it around the little boy and hugged him tightly. "Are you OK?"

Brian nodded and hiccupped.

"He's more scared than hurt," Enid observed. "Kevin got there just in time."

After ordering the rest of the campers out of the water, the other counselors gathered around Kevin. Jessica, apparently having forgotten that only a few minutes earlier she'd been sulking about Kevin's attentions to Elizabeth, flung her arms around him. "You're a hero!" she exclaimed.

"You saved Brian's life," Cara said emotionally.

Kyle pounded Kevin on the back. "Great

swimming," he praised. "I wish I'd had a stop-watch on you."

"I never had such a good incentive to swim so fast," Kevin declared, shaking the water out of his hair. His pale eyes found Todd. "I'm just glad I was keeping my eye on the Eagles as well as the Otters. What were *you* looking at, Wilkins?"

Todd had been determined to keep quiet while the others made a big deal over Kevin, but Kevin's baiting remark stung him out of his silence. "I *was* watching my campers," Todd retorted angrily. "I was in control of the situation. But you had to turn the rescue into a competition, didn't you? Well, you won. I hope you're happy."

Kevin raised his eyebrows, as if he were as astonished as everybody else at Todd's violent reaction.

The other counselors stared at Todd. He saw the condemnation in their eyes, even in Elizabeth's, and cringed. He knew he was lying. He hadn't been watching his campers closely enough; he hadn't been in control of the situation.

Todd knew how his behavior must look to the other counselors. They probably thought he was jealous of the attention Kevin was getting. Melissa confirmed this. "I can't believe you could care who actually made the rescue!" she said.

Ed frowned. "Yeah, what matters is that the kid was saved."

Todd gritted his teeth. He wanted to set the matter straight, but he couldn't. He couldn't tell Ed and the others that Kevin was manipulating him again. Once more Kevin had made himself look good at Todd's expense.

"I know what matters," Todd said quietly. He retrieved his sunglasses, then signaled to his cluster. "Let's go, kids!" Todd held out a hand to Brian. "You, too, pal."

Brian shook his head. "I want to be an Otter," he announced, trotting over to Kevin's side.

Kevin grinned at Todd. "He can be an Otter until his mom comes to pick him up. I'll take care of him."

Todd nodded curtly, turned, and strode off toward the lodge.

He knew as soon as his back was turned the other counselors would start talking about him. *It doesn't matter*, Todd told himself as his cluster disappeared into the changing rooms to get out of their wet swimsuits. It didn't matter if the Fort Carroll and Big Mesa kids—Melissa, Ed, Jill, and Kyle—had gotten a bad impression of him.

A bad impression . . . Todd smiled bitterly to himself as he closed the changing-room door behind him. *Face it, Wilkins. They think you're a real jerk!*

Each changing room had a small screened

ventilation window high up on the wall. As Todd was tying his sneakers, he heard two people speaking in hushed tones outside the lodge. He recognized the voices immediately as belonging to Aaron and Winston.

"You saw what just happened," Aaron said. "Todd was totally out of line. He's got some kind of grudge against Kevin."

"It doesn't make sense." Winston sounded puzzled. "I mean, Kevin's a perfectly good guy. What reason could Todd have for giving him the cold shoulder?"

Todd could almost picture Aaron giving a shrug. "I don't know," Aaron said after a thoughtful pause. "Maybe he's just being a snob."

"Todd's not a snob," Winston protested.

"I don't like to think that, either," Aaron said. "But remember the way he acted when he first moved back from Vermont, hanging out with the country-club crowd? Maybe he looks down on Kevin for some reason."

Winston sighed. "Maybe. I just don't get it."

"Hey, Winston, Aaron." Todd recognized Cara's voice now. "Have either of you guys seen my keys? They're on a chain with a Lucite frame with Steven's picture in it. I thought I put them in my beach bag but I can't find them anywhere. . . ." The voices trailed off as Cara, Aaron, and Winston moved away from the lodge.

Todd had been holding his breath. Now he let it out in a sigh as heavy as Winston's. What he had heard really hurt. But he knew he couldn't blame Aaron and Winston for talking about him. They could only judge him from what they'd seen of his behavior.

Todd joined his campers outside the lodge. As the kids waited for their rides home, the counselors mingled and chatted. No one approached Todd. Even Elizabeth kept her distance, although at one point Todd caught her looking at him, a pained expression on her face. As soon as his eyes met hers, she looked quickly away. Loneliness washed over him. He was in trouble with his fellow counselors, and it wasn't much better at home; his father was still irked over Todd's rash accusation of Kevin.

Never in his life had Todd felt like such an outsider. It was a new, and unpleasant, experience. Meanwhile, Kevin had never been so popular. Todd could see him at the center of a laughing group. It was as if their roles had been reversed. Was this part of Kevin's plan for revenge?

Nine

Elizabeth stood at the edge of the Secca Lake parking lot and watched Todd drive off.

"He sure left in a hurry," Kevin said amiably.

"When doesn't he?" remarked Melissa with more than a hint of sarcasm.

Elizabeth bit her lip and turned to face the other camp counselors. Everyone had decided to go to Guido's Pizza Palace to celebrate Kevin's heroism, but Todd had declined to join them. She was painfully conscious that Todd's antisocial behavior, especially after what happened that day, made him look particularly bad. Of course no one had actually said anything to her, but Elizabeth had picked up on the fact that the others thought Todd was a snob and a bad sport.

Elizabeth glanced at Winston and Aaron in

time to see the two boys exchange a troubled glance. Apparently they, too, had noticed Todd's strange behavior lately. But neither of them spoke up in his defense.

"Just as well," Ed observed dryly. "Wilkins is such a cutthroat competitive type, he probably couldn't just relax and eat normally. He'd have to turn it into a pizza-eating contest."

Kevin laughed. "You're right, it's just as well. I'm the former pizza-eating champion of Vermont! C'mon, let's go."

The counselors split up and headed for their cars. Jessica tagged after Kevin. Enid was the only one who saw the angry blush spread across Elizabeth's face. "Kevin and Ed were just kidding around," Enid said to Elizabeth as the two girls climbed into the twins' new Jeep.

"Oh, I'm not mad at them," Elizabeth explained. "I'm not mad at anybody but Todd. He's got no one but himself to blame if the rest of the counselors, at least those who don't go to Sweet Valley High, think he's a jerk!"

"I wouldn't exactly say they think he's a jerk," Enid protested.

"Well, they don't like him," Elizabeth said bluntly. "I know what people are saying behind Todd's back, and behind mine. Even Winston and Aaron are turned off by the way Todd's been acting lately." Elizabeth pounded her fist against the steering wheel. "It just makes me so mad!" she burst out. "Todd's such a good person. What's eating him? Why is he doing this to himself?"

"We hashed this out a hundred times this past weekend," Enid reminded Elizabeth, "and we didn't come to any very satisfying conclusions. Although we did manage to polish off a few dozen chocolate-chip cookies and almost a gallon of ice cream!"

Elizabeth smiled weakly. It was true. As usual, Enid had been there when Elizabeth needed her, ready with cookies, ice cream, and advice. "Whatever his problem is, it's not my business anymore. I'm not going to worry about him. He made his choice, right? He's choosing not to share anything with me. There's nothing I can do."

"You *did* do something, though," Enid said as Elizabeth backed the Jeep out of the parking space. "You could've let things slide and lived with the fact that Todd wasn't giving his share to your relationship. Instead you took a positive step to change things."

Elizabeth forced a smile. "I never thought I'd consider breaking up with Todd a positive step!"

"It will be positive if it shakes him up and brings you two closer together, which is what I think is going to happen," Enid predicted encouragingly. "Just be patient, Liz. Give him the benefit of the doubt."

Elizabeth drove away from Secca Lake toward downtown Sweet Valley. Knowing

123

she'd done the right thing was only the faintest consolation. It didn't relieve her loneliness one little bit.

She pulled up in front of Guido's and reluctantly turned off the Jeep's engine. "I'm not really in the mood for pizza," she confessed.

Enid nodded sympathetically; what Elizabeth meant was she wasn't in the mood to hang around with the other counselors, knowing how they felt about Todd. "We don't have to stay long," Enid pointed out. "Just long enough to eat a couple of slices—pepperoni with extra cheese."

The other counselors were already squeezed around a big round table. Elizabeth was glad to see there was no more room at the table. She and Enid had an excuse to leave.

But Kevin stood up as Elizabeth and Enid approached. "We can't leave you two out. Enid, you sit here. Liz and I can grab that table over there."

Jessica, who'd been sitting next to Kevin, glowered at Elizabeth. Elizabeth shrugged helplessly. She wasn't seeking special attention from Kevin; she certainly didn't intend to trespass on her twin's romantic territory. There wasn't anything she could do, though, but follow Kevin to the small table he'd staked out.

As they sat down a waitress arrived with the large Italian sub Kevin had ordered. "I'll just have a soda," Elizabeth told her.

"We can split my sub," Kevin offered.

"No, go ahead. I'm not hungry."

"Really, I can spare some of it," he insisted. "Because I also ordered a large pepperoni pizza to go."

Elizabeth laughed. "That's right, you're cooking for yourself these days. You must miss living at home with your parents, huh?"

Kevin's smile faded and he narrowed his eyes. "Not a—yeah. Yeah, I do miss home." His smile returned, brighter than ever. He cut off a small piece of the sandwich for Elizabeth. "Not as much as they miss me, though. You know how it is." Kevin winked at her. "I'm an only child, so naturally they make a big deal over me."

"An only child," Elizabeth mused. For a moment she was puzzled. Hadn't Jessica told her that Kevin had a brother? She must have gotten the story wrong. Elizabeth nibbled at the sub. "I suppose your dad wants you to take over his company some day."

"Of course," Kevin said breezily. "Isn't that what any normal father would want for his son?"

Elizabeth thought about Todd and Mr. Wilkins. She nodded. "But some parents expect too much. There can be too much pressure on an only child to fulfill all of his parents' dreams. I know Todd feels really burdened sometimes."

Kevin laughed harshly. "Poor Todd. So he complains because his parents pay too much attention to him? How would he like it if his

125

parents didn't care what he did or where he went, if they wished they had *no* kids instead of just one if that one had to be *him*?"

Elizabeth felt as if she was sitting across the table from a total stranger. Kevin's eyes had frozen into pale green ice; his mouth had hardened into a thin, angry line.

What is this all about? Elizabeth wondered. Suddenly she didn't think Kevin was so handsome; she didn't even think he was nice. An unexpected thought struck her. Maybe Todd was right. Maybe Kevin wasn't such a great guy after all.

Elizabeth opened her mouth to ask Kevin what he'd meant by his outburst, and then closed it. Kevin was smiling again. It was as if a mask had slipped off his face. Or had it slipped back on? "Come on, Liz," he said playfully. "I don't want to have to force-feed you. Dig into that sub."

Elizabeth took a bite of the sub, not because she was hungry but in order to hide her confusion. Once again Kevin's eyes were warm, friendly, admiring. How could they ever have appeared otherwise?

Of course, Elizabeth told herself. *Kevin was kidding around. I can't let Todd's bad attitude rub off on me. I'm free to make my own judgment of Kevin. And I like him.*

Kevin leaned close to Elizabeth. "How about it, Liz?" he said, his voice caressing and his smile flirtatious. "Will you let me take you out for a real meal one of these days?"

Elizabeth was surprised. Kevin was asking her for a date. Her first instinct was to turn him down. With her heart aching over Todd, Elizabeth knew she couldn't enjoy herself with another boy, particularly a boy her own sister was very interested in. At the same time, it seemed cruel to reject Kevin outright. Elizabeth thought about all the trouble Todd had been causing at camp; Kevin deserved a warmer welcome to Sweet Valley. Really, she decided, if all Kevin wanted was her friendship, the least she could do was give him a chance. Maybe she could make up to him for Todd's hostility.

Jessica's probably going to kill me. Elizabeth returned Kevin's smile. "A meal one of these days would be great."

Todd's parents had already left the house when he came downstairs on Tuesday morning. Todd settled down at the table with a pitcher of fresh-squeezed orange juice, a plate of toast, and the *Sweet Valley News*. After checking the scores in the sports section, Todd turned to the front page. As he scanned the headlines, one in particular grabbed his attention.

Todd read quickly. According to the article, Mr. Caster, an elderly man who owned a bakery downtown, had been beaten and robbed on a quiet Sweet Valley side street the previous night. Mr. Caster hadn't gotten a good look at his assailant, and the police had no leads.

Key words and phrases jumped off the page as Todd stared at the article. *Assault and robbery . . . first such incident in Sweet Valley in years . . . attacker remains at large . . .*

Todd bit into a piece of toast. In spite of the strawberry jam, it tasted as dry as dust. A terrible suspicion forced its way into his mind. The mugging—could Kevin have been responsible? No, Todd told himself sternly. Just because Kevin was renting an apartment only a couple of blocks from where the mugging occurred, didn't mean he was guilty.

Tood grabbed the pitcher, poured himself a glass of juice, and gulped it down. He read the story again, making an effort to remain calm and unprejudiced. Muggings were uncommon in Sweet Valley, but that was no reason to suspect Kevin. He folded the newspaper and tossed it on the table. "It probably wasn't Kevin," he said out loud. *It probably wasn't. But what if it was?*

And what about Elizabeth? Todd gripped the edge of the table. His hands were shaking. He fought an urge to jump in his car and race over to her house. *I'll see her in half an hour*, he reassured himself. He couldn't approach her, talk to her, or touch her, but at least he could see her.

128

Yes, he'd see her—hanging out with Kevin Holmes! Todd was beginning to wish he'd never seen the newspaper article. What was the point of speculating about Kevin being the mugger? Todd couldn't do anything about it. He had no proof of any wrongdoing on Kevin's part, only the threats. It would be Todd's word against Kevin's.

More than ever, Todd felt his hands were tied. Because if Kevin wasn't bluffing about hurting someone Todd cared about, if it *had* been Kevin who mugged Mr. Caster, then Todd could be risking Elizabeth's life if he blew Kevin's cover now.

Todd thought about old Mr. Caster, and then again about Elizabeth. He could see no clear solution, no matter how he looked at the situation. It all came back to the unknown quantity that was Kevin Holmes. Who *was* Kevin Holmes? What was he after? What was going to happen next? Todd had only one option: to wait and see. But he wasn't sure he could hold out for much longer.

"There goes Todd, by himself again," observed Cara. She shook her head. "He's really turning into a hermit."

Jessica and Cara were spending Tuesday's lunch break working on their tans with Lila, who'd come to Secca Lake as a change of pace from the ocean and the pool in her backyard.

Jessica shaded her eyes with the copy of the *Sweet Valley News* Lila had brought with her. Todd was walking along the lakeshore, his back to the world. "Hermit's putting it too nicely, if you ask me," Jessica declared. "Try antisocial loser."

"Jessica! How can you say that about your sister's boyfriend?" demanded Cara.

"Her ex-boyfriend," Jessica corrected her. "Liz sure did the right thing, telling him to bug off."

"I thought this breakup thing was just temporary," Lila drawled.

"Maybe, maybe not." Jessica opened the newspaper. "Don't get me wrong, guys. I always liked Todd. But now I'm starting to think Liz would have been better off sticking with Jeffrey French instead of getting back with Todd when he moved back from Vermont."

"Do you really think Todd's changed that much?" asked Cara. "Maybe he's just got a lot on his mind."

"He *has* changed," Jessica insisted. "We just couldn't see it at first because we've known him for so long. But Kevin and Melissa and Ed and Kyle and Jill didn't know him at all before. Their opinion of Todd is closer to the truth."

Cara looked a little confused by Jessica's reasoning. "Well, maybe. They're not exactly wild about him, that's for sure."

"Of course they're not. He's totally unfriendly

toward them, especially Kevin." Jessica reached into Lila's beach bag for a bottle of suntan lotion. "Liz can definitely do better."

"You'd just better watch out she doesn't do better by stealing Kevin away from you!" Lila said slyly. "I heard about what happened at Guido's last night."

Jessica frowned. Lila certainly knew how to hit a person where it hurt. It hadn't been a pretty sight, watching Elizabeth and Kevin cuddle up at a tiny table for two. "There's no *stealing* going on," Jessica said firmly, as much to convince herself as Lila. "Kevin just feels sorry for Elizabeth because she broke up with Todd."

Lila grinned. "Whatever you say, Jess!"

"What were you saying?"

Jessica looked up. Kevin was standing by her towel, smiling down at her. "What was I saying?" She racked her brains for a topic. Then she glanced down, and a *Sweet Valley News* headline caught her eye. "I was just saying how awful it is that Mr. Caster, the baker, got mugged last night."

Winston, Aaron, Melissa, and Kyle came up behind Kevin. They all sat down on the sand by the three girls. Kevin raised his eyebrows. "Somebody got mugged? Here in Sweet Valley?"

"Check out the paper." Winston tapped the front page. "A really bad scene. Mr. Caster's the nicest old guy."

"He also has the best bakery in southern California," Cara contributed.

Aaron scowled. "I just hate to think of some-one beating up on a harmless old man. What kind of person would do something like that?"

Kevin shook his head. "You got me."

Jessica was gazing raptly at Kevin's picture-perfect profile; she didn't notice Todd until Aaron waved at him. Todd lifted his hand in a half-wave, but instead of joining the group, he headed back in the direction of Secca Lodge.

"I tried, didn't I?" Aaron said to Winston.

"You tried," Winston confirmed with a sigh.

"I can't figure him out, you know?" Aaron's tone was frustrated. "For the past couple of weeks he just hasn't been himself."

"I don't know about that," said Kevin. "He seems to be acting just like he did when he lived in Burlington."

"But you said you two didn't know each other in Vermont!" Jessica exclaimed.

Kevin's expression grew sheepish. "I didn't really know Todd," he said quickly. "Forget it."

"Hold it, Holmes," Aaron said. "If you've got something to say about Todd, say it. We're his friends. We'd like to know."

"I guess I might as well tell the whole story," Kevin said reluctantly.

Jessica inched closer to him on the sand. "The whole story?" she prompted eagerly.

"Like I said, I didn't know Todd in Bur-lington," Kevin began. "But I knew *of* him. Todd wasn't at the high school long before he had a reputation."

"What kind of reputation?" asked Winston.

"People thought he was a bully."

Jessica glanced at Lila and then at Cara and saw her astonishment mirrored in her friends' eyes. Todd might be a lot of things, but a bully?

"He roughed up a couple of basketball players from a rival school," Kevin continued. "Once he even punched out a guy on his own team."

"I don't believe it," Aaron exclaimed. "Todd would never do that!"

"I believe it," Kyle interjected. "I've seen him on the basketball court here at the camp. He's a madman."

"I wish it weren't true," Kevin said apologetically. "And I wish that was the worst of it."

"You mean there's more?" Melissa added.

Kevin lowered his voice. "There was an . . . incident with a girl. A girl Todd took out on a date. Nobody knows exactly what happened." Kevin paused significantly. "But she had to jump out of his car to get away from him. She walked home."

Jessica's mouth had gone dry. At that moment, she was relieved that her sister had broke up with Todd.

"I'm sorry, you guys," Kevin said. "Sorry to be the bearer of bad news. But you should know the truth about your friend. I guess it just goes to show that sometimes you don't know a person as well as you think you do."

He looked at his watch and then hopped to

his feet. "Time to get back to the little monsters."

Kyle and Melissa hurried off with Kevin, leaving Jessica, Cara, Lila, Winston, and Aaron staring at one another in stunned silence. "I can't believe it," Winston said at last.

"Maybe Kevin has it wrong," Cara said hopefully.

"He sounded as if he knew what he was talking about," Aaron observed, his expression grim.

"You could tell he hated to have to be the one to tell us," said Jessica, a chill running down her spine.

"He didn't *sound* as if he was lying," put in Lila, who was an expert at the art.

"No, he's not lying," Aaron agreed. "He'd have no reason to lie."

For a long moment the five were silent, each absorbed in his or her own thoughts. "I just can't believe it," Winston finally repeated.

"You mean, you don't *want* to believe it," Aaron said. "Well, neither do I."

"But when you think about it, it is kind of strange," Winston began slowly. "I mean, the way Todd and his family moved back to Sweet Valley so suddenly."

"Do you think it was more than just Mr. Wilkins's promotion?" Cara speculated. "Maybe Mr. Wilkins asked for a transfer because Todd was having problems adjusting?"

"Kevin knows *something* about Todd, that

much is for sure," Aaron asserted. "Why else would Todd be acting so hostile toward him?"

Cara's and Aaron's suggestions left Jessica speechless. She felt sick to her stomach. Did Todd really have a cruel side to his character that she—and Elizabeth—knew nothing about?

Todd had certainly never told Elizabeth about these scrapes in Vermont. And Jessica knew that even though they were separated, Elizabeth still considered Todd a knight in shining armor. *But he's no knight*, Jessica thought. *He's a bully— and possibly worse.*

"Are you going to tell Liz?" Lila asked Jessica.

Jessica lifted her shoulders helplessly. "Do you think I should?" Jessica hated to imagine how much the information would hurt Elizabeth. "It would upset her so much."

"Maybe there's no need to," Cara suggested. "Liz isn't in any danger from Todd as long as she's not seeing him. I mean, if Todd *is* dangerous, which I really don't think he is," she added hastily.

Jessica nodded unhappily. Cara was right. As long as Elizabeth and Todd were separated, Elizabeth wasn't in any immediate danger. But if they should decide to get back together, Jessica knew she'd have no choice. As difficult as it would be, she'd have to set her sister straight.

Ten

It had been another endless day for Todd. Could it really have been only that morning that he'd read about the mugging? Todd felt as if he'd been living with the unnerving possibility of Kevin's guilt for a decade.

From the blacktopped area where he was coaching basketball, Todd glanced across the lawn to where Kevin and Jessica were refereeing an energetic soccer match. Jessica was as relaxed and happy as she could be around Kevin; it wasn't lost on Todd that she was giving *him* the cold shoulder. Todd supposed she had good reason; he'd caused her sister pain. And Jessica wasn't the only one treating him strangely. The other counselors had closed up their circle. Even Winston and Aaron preferred to hang around with Kevin than with him.

When the soccer game was over, Todd sent his basketball players to join the other kids. Jessica got the whole group started playing duck-duck-goose, a good way to kill the last ten minutes of the day.

Kevin sauntered across the grass toward Todd. When he reached the blacktop, he scooped up a basketball. "Don't suppose you're up for a little one-on-one," he joked, slapping Todd on the shoulder in a jovial manner.

"No, thanks," Todd replied coldly.

"Speaking of thanks, I've been meaning to thank *you*," Kevin said as he bounced the basketball. His face creased in the sly grin he seemed to save for Todd. "Thanks for freeing up Elizabeth so the rest of us can have a chance with her."

Todd clenched his fists. "Stay away from her, Holmes."

"Don't see why I should," Kevin drawled. "She's a gorgeous girl. Besides, she's capable of choosing her own friends, don't you think?"

"She doesn't know any better," Todd answered bitterly.

Kevin laughed. "It's true. She doesn't. No one around here seems to know any better. What sheltered lives you've all led. But Sweet Valley's not such an idyllic place after all, is it, Wilkins?"

Todd frowned. "What do you mean?"

"Just that I thought I was moving to a safe little town. But I hear there was an *incident.*

Looks like life in Sweet Valley could turn out to be as dangerous as life in Burlington, eh?"

Kevin's eyes were as hard and opaque as stones. Todd couldn't penetrate them; he couldn't detect any emotion behind them. There was only Kevin's grin, his perverse amusement.

Kevin was talking about the mugging. To anyone else his remark might have seemed innocuous, but to Todd it was the equivalent of an explicit admission of guilt. *Kevin beat up Mr. Caster*, Todd thought with disgust. *Kevin stalked a helpless old man down a dark street, knocked him down, and stole his money.* Worst of all, Kevin showed no remorse. If anything, Todd judged, he was exulting in the fact that he'd gotten away with it, and that Todd was being forced against his will to act as an accessory to the crime.

"I know what you're thinking." Kevin lowered his voice. "I can read you like a book, Wilkins. It's written all over your pathetically noble face. You think you should turn me in. But you're not going to. And you know why?"

Todd didn't speak. Kevin was playing with him, torturing him, and he had to endure it.

"That's right," Kevin said. "Because what happened to Mr. Caster could happen to anybody. It could happen to someone *you* care about."

"No," Todd said hoarsely.

"It *could* happen to someone you care about, Wilkins, but it won't. I know I can trust you to keep quiet." Kevin sneered. "When it comes down to it, we're a lot alike, you and I."

"No!" Todd repeated desperately.

Kevin's smile was soft and evil. "Yes," he insisted. Then he turned and walked away, leaving Todd alone with the terrible thought.

When it comes down to it, we're a lot alike. Todd glanced over at Kevin, Jessica, and the children playing duck-duck-goose. *Is Kevin right? Because I didn't expose him, and I'm not going to, am I equally responsible for the mugging? Am I as much of a coward and a thief as Kevin?*

The agonizing questions cut to the core of Todd's being. Maybe he *was* no better a person than Kevin Holmes.

Thank goodness this day is over, Elizabeth thought as the last of her cluster left for home. Keeping a smile on her face for hours on end was a terrible strain. All she really wanted to do was go home and hide from the world.

As she walked back toward the lodge, Elizabeth was joined by Enid. "Think positive," Enid urged her friend. "You're not a victim, remember? You're in control of your life and it's going to be better because you took a stand with Todd about your relationship."

Elizabeth smiled wryly at Enid. "OK, I confess. You caught me feeling sorry for myself. But you know, Enid, that's not the worst part." A preoccupied frown creased Elizabeth's forehead. "Before, I was just upset for myself, because I didn't understand Todd and I thought he was treating me unfairly. But now, more than anything else, I'm worried about him."

"He's acting more strangely all the time," Enid concurred.

"I thought our talk last week would mark some kind of turning point," Elizabeth said. "I thought by taking some kind of drastic action, I'd finally get through to him. But he hasn't made any move to bridge the gap between us." Elizabeth shivered. She felt as if the sun had slipped behind a cloud, leaving the world cold and lonely. "It's getting wider every day."

"He's distant with everyone," Enid remarked. "He hardly says a word to me."

"When he does say something," Elizabeth continued, "it's something negative or confrontational. He's just plain irritable."

"He's edgy, all right," Enid agreed.

"But it all comes back to the same thing!" Elizabeth declared. "It's up to him to come to me. I can't help unless he asks me to." *And I can't love him unless he lets me*, she added silently.

Elizabeth and Enid rounded the side of the lodge and almost stumbled over Jessica, Cara, Aaron, and Winston, who were standing in a tight huddle. When the four saw Elizabeth and Enid, they jumped apart guiltily.

"What's the gossip?" Enid asked lightly.

Jessica shot a glance at Winston, Aaron, and Cara. "No gossip," Jessica said quickly. "We were just talking about, uh, playing badminton. Kevin and Ed are setting up a couple of nets on the beach. Want to join us?"

"Actually, I was thinking about heading home," Elizabeth told her sister.

Jessica elbowed Winston in the side to let him know she expected him to back her up.

"No, you're not. You have to stick around and be my partner," Winston insisted, grabbing Elizabeth's arm and steering her toward the beach. "I promise you, we'll go places."

Elizabeth laughed. "I bet."

Jessica helped hustle Elizabeth onto the sand. "Here," she said, sticking a badminton racket in Elizabeth's hand. She gave Winston a shove. "Go play with the guys," she hissed at him. Then she turned back to Elizabeth. "Me and Cara against you and Enid."

At that moment Ed, who was standing by the other badminton net with Kevin and Aaron, gave a shout. "My watch is gone!" He picked up a T-shirt that had been lying on the sand and shook it out. "I put it right on top of my shirt a few minutes ago. Did anybody see it?"

Jessica and the other counselors spent a minute dutifully scanning the sand, but to no avail.

"Are you sure you didn't leave it somewhere

else?" Kevin asked Ed. "I mean, a wristwatch just doesn't get up and walk away."

Ed wrinkled his nose. "I'm almost positive. I could have sworn . . . but maybe not."

"You probably left it in the lodge," Jessica said dismissively. She really didn't care about Ed's lost watch. She was thinking about the conversation she, Cara, Aaron, and Winston had been having when Elizabeth and Enid interrupted them a few minutes earlier. Winston and Aaron were reporting on a sort of test they'd given Todd. As soon as camp let out, Todd's friends had cornered him and urged him to stick around for a while. Pretending they just wanted to shoot the breeze, Aaron and Winston had asked some questions about Vermont to see if Todd would say anything that might prove or disprove Kevin's disturbing allegations. To their dismay, Todd had changed the subject immediately. He refused to talk about his life in Vermont.

It had been all the proof Jessica needed. As much as she and the rest of the gang might hate to admit it, it looked as if Kevin was telling the truth about Todd. Which didn't leave them a choice, in Jessica's opinion. If it weren't for Todd's connection to Elizabeth, Jessica might have considered giving him the benefit of the doubt. But Elizabeth came first. She had to be protected.

Jessica grabbed a birdie and hit it over the

net to Elizabeth, simultaneously launching into a not-so-subtle campaign to talk down Todd and to convince her twin to make the breakup permanent.

"This is the best part of the day, when the kids go home. Yep, that's when the fun starts," Jessica babbled. "Too bad Todd never sticks around. Or maybe it's not too bad. You know, he's still giving Kevin a hard time about saving that little boy's life? I overheard him saying some really mean things to Kevin." Lying in a situation like this didn't make Jessica feel at all guilty. In her opinion, a lie wasn't really a lie if you told it for a good purpose, *and* if it sounded plausible. "He said some nasty things and then he kind of gave Kevin a shove," she went on, getting carried away by her story.

On the other side of the net, Elizabeth and Enid exchanged shocked glances.

"Back me up, Cara," Jessica whispered.

"I can't lie like that," Cara whispered back. "Can't we use another strategy?"

"No. Now back me up!" Jessica hissed.

Cara swallowed her guilt. "I saw it, too," she piped up, taking a swipe at the birdie. "Todd acted like a total bully. He's obviously jealous of Kevin's popularity."

"I always thought Todd was kind of arrogant," Jessica continued. "No doubt about it, Liz, you dumped him in the nick of time."

"You deserve better," Cara asserted.

"That's right," Jessica concurred, darting to the left to return a wild shot from Elizabeth. "And you know who was asking me about you today? Kyle." This was another lie, but Jessica saw no reason to stop now. Jessica could tell by Elizabeth's expression that the plan to disillusion her and steer her in new directions was working.

"He's got a major crush on you," Cara added.

"He's cute," Jessica gushed.

"I'd go for it if I were you," said Cara, tapping the birdie over the net to Elizabeth.

Elizabeth took a swing at the birdie and missed. Jessica pressed her advantage. "*Todd's* not wasting any time moving on, that's for sure," she said.

Elizabeth spoke for the first time since the badminton game had begun. "What do you mean?" she demanded.

Jessica put her hand over her mouth as if she'd let a secret slip out. "I wasn't going to say anything but supposedly Todd's been putting the moves on, uh . . ." Jessica paused. Jill or Melissa? Jessica had never seen Todd talking to either of them. "On some girl from the country club," she improvised. "Lila told me. Maybe that's why he doesn't hang around after camp."

Elizabeth's cheeks flushed a deep pink. "I

don't think I'll play anymore," she said quietly. Dropping her badminton racket on the sand, she turned and walked away.

Enid hurried after her. Jessica sighed deeply and looked after them. She hated to hurt her twin, but she had to be cruel to be kind. It was the only way.

Eleven

Todd knew that getting so little sleep didn't help his frame of mind. But he seemed to be turning into an insomniac. On Wednesday morning, he woke up long before dawn and couldn't doze off again. Finally, he got up and got dressed. He might as well head to Secca Lake.

His was the first car in the parking lot. In the pink rays of the newly risen sun, the beach was peaceful; only seagulls scurried along the lake's edge, dodging the lapping waves.

Todd sat on the sand and let his mind wander. The minutes passed by and his thoughts chased themselves in circles as erratic as the gulls'. When had he stopped living his own life? When and how had he lost control and become Kevin's puppet?

Todd heard voices behind him. He checked his watch and discovered it was 7:45. He'd been sitting by the shore for more than an hour.

Todd turned his head slightly and saw a group of counselors, Elizabeth among them, walking in his direction. They were chatting animatedly; Elizabeth was carrying a bag from Caster's bakery. Todd expected them to give him a wide berth; instead, with Kevin leading the way, they stopped only a yard away from him.

Before she sat down with the others, Elizabeth held out the bakery bag to Todd. "Want a donut?" she asked, at the same time avoiding his eyes.

Todd flushed and reached into the bag. He didn't want a donut; he wanted Elizabeth. But he couldn't speak to her, and she wouldn't look at him.

Winston bit into a jelly donut. "I can't believe it," he exclaimed. His tone was serious, but with powdered sugar all over his face he looked comical. "In all the years I've lived in Sweet Valley, I don't think anybody has ever been mugged. And now it happens two nights in a row."

Two nights in a row? Todd sat up straighter. A feeling of dread washed over him. He'd left the house before the morning paper had been delivered. What had he missed?

Enid asked the question for him. "Was there another mugging? What happened? I didn't see the newspaper."

"It was a woman this time," Aaron told Enid. "A purse snatching. The mugger broke the woman's wrist in the process."

A sick, defeated feeling settled in Todd's stomach. Another mugging, and the horrifying thing was that he wasn't even surprised that Kevin had struck again, or that Kevin should be sitting within feet of him, calmly eating donuts.

"Do you think it was the same person who robbed Mr. Caster?" Cara wondered.

"It has to be," Jessica said.

"It was the same sort of crime," Winston observed. "Approximately the same time of night *and* only one street from where Mr. Caster was mugged."

"Did the woman get a look at who attacked her?" Kevin asked.

"According to the story in the paper, no," Elizabeth answered. "It was after dark and the guy came up behind her. He grabbed the purse and ran off before she knew what had happened."

Kevin bent over the bag to select another donut. "It's really a shame," he said solemnly. "But the police are bound to catch the mugger. He won't get away with it forever."

Todd remained on the outer edge of the circle of counselors, an untasted donut in his hand, and felt himself grow more and more numb. *This isn't happening*, he told himself. *It's just not real.*

It was like watching a movie. Elizabeth and

Jessica and the others were just reading from a script. And Kevin was the best actor of all. So smooth, so calm, sounding as puzzled and concerned as everybody else. But he'd mugged that woman, and Mr. Caster. Hadn't he?

Todd put his hand to his eyes and rubbed them hard. He wanted to be able to see the truth; he wanted to know. *I don't know, though.* Granted, Kevin had threatened Todd, and yesterday Kevin had practically boasted that he was responsible for the first mugging. But maybe boasting was all it was. Todd had no evidence that Kevin had actually done anything wrong. No evidence, Todd thought, just this mounting sense of crisis, this feeling that he was losing control over his life—losing himself. The feeling that he didn't know what was going to happen next, or worse, that he did know but was powerless to affect events. And while Todd found himself slipping, he saw Kevin settling in, secure in his new friendships, Mr. Schiavitti's pet counselor, practically a surrogate son of Todd's own father.

As he studied Kevin, Todd abruptly changed his mind. Kevin couldn't have committed the crimes. It simply wasn't possible. He couldn't have mugged somebody last night and this morning be entirely composed. If he were the mugger, wouldn't he be a bundle of nerves? Wouldn't he give himself away? Wouldn't everyone know just by looking at him that he was guilty? No, Kevin must be innocent, Todd decided. A person simply couldn't be one thing on the outside and something entirely different on the inside.

So what does that say about me? Todd looked down at his hands. Kevin's hands didn't appear to be shaking, but his were. Todd tightened them into fists and shoved them into his pockets.

"What do you think, Todd?"

Todd jerked his head up. Aaron seemed to be tossing out the question in a friendly effort to include him in the conversation. "What?" He looked blankly at Aaron, then at Elizabeth. Once again she averted her gaze.

Todd knew he couldn't participate casually in this discussion; he was by no means sure he could maintain his self-control. "Oh, I, uh, I didn't get a chance to read the paper this morning. This is the first I've heard of it." He jumped to his feet. "Got some things to do before the kids get here," he mumbled.

He could feel the other counselors' eyes on him as he walked away.

Inside Secca Lodge, Todd dropped onto one of the pine benches and buried his face in his hands. Camp, and his problem with Kevin, had been going on for only a week and a half. How could his relationship to the world around him, and his sense of himself, have changed so much in so little time?

Todd sat in the empty lodge, weighed down by his aloneness. He'd always had faith in his own values and strength, but now, when he needed them most, they seemed to be deserting him. And now, when more than ever in his life he needed someone to talk to, he had no one. The people he wanted to lean on—his father and Elizabeth—were out of reach.

What is Kevin doing to my life? Todd asked himself in despair. *And why is he doing it? When—and how— will this end?*

Elizabeth hadn't intended to accept Kevin's invitation when he approached her Wednesday afternoon. She wasn't sure why Kevin had decided to pursue her instead of Jessica, but she did know that Jessica was peeved about it. She'd begun to regret having encouraged Kevin the other night at Guido's. She had no special interest in Kevin, or in any other boy for that matter. Cara and Jessica's gossip about Kyle having a crush on her hadn't touched her at all. Elizabeth had determined that when Kevin did ask her to dinner, she would send a very clear, discouraging message. She hoped that once he realized she wasn't interested, he'd turn his attention back to Jessica.

Kevin had caught up with Elizabeth in the lodge, where she was putting away some books on bird identification. "Hey, Liz, remember you promised you'd let me take you out to dinner sometime?"

At that moment the door to Secca Lodge had

swung open and Todd walked in carrying a bag full of softball equipment.

"How about tonight?" Kevin had continued. "I've been hearing good things about the Box Tree Café. Will you let me take you there?"

Elizabeth's cheeks had burned. She'd been painfully aware that Todd could hear every word she and Kevin exchanged. Kevin hadn't seemed fazed by that; he'd actually sent a smile in Todd's direction.

"Tonight? Well, I—" Elizabeth had been ready to make an excuse. Then she had looked across the lodge and tried to meet Todd's eyes.

If he'd appeared in the least bit hurt, she would have stuck to her original intention and turned Kevin down. Instead, Todd's expression, turned on Kevin rather than Elizabeth, had been angry and bitter. *He doesn't care about me*, she had realized with a stab of pain. All the things Jessica and Cara had told her about Todd the day before, things Elizabeth had been trying not to dwell on, had rushed back into her mind. *He only cares about his infantile competition with Kevin. He doesn't want me himself, he just doesn't want Kevin to have me. And what about that girl from the country club?*

"I'd love to have dinner with you tonight," Elizabeth had declared.

Kevin had flashed her a delighted smile; Todd's expression had darkened further. Elizabeth had never felt so confused and uncomfortable.

Now, at home, Elizabeth was looking out her bedroom window for Kevin's sporty black Mazda. She was hoping to sneak out without Jessica noticing and avoid a confrontation. She might be able to swing it. Lila was visiting; between the stereo blasting and their own gabbing, there was a good chance Jessica and Lila wouldn't hear the car in the driveway.

The instant the Mazda appeared, Elizabeth dashed out into the hallway. She almost collided with Jessica and Lila, who'd burst out of Jessica's room at the same time.

"Did you see who just pulled in?" Jessica squealed. She fluffed her loose blond hair with her fingers. "Don't bother, I'll get the door."

"Uh, Jess—"

"I can't believe he's just stopping by like this, out of the blue!"

"He must really be smitten," Lila said enviously.

Jessica was preparing to bound down the stairs. Elizabeth blocked her path. "He's not just stopping by," Elizabeth announced. "He's picking me up. We're going out to dinner."

Jessica's blue eyes widened in disbelief. "He's picking you up for dinner? He's picking *you* up?"

Elizabeth nodded apologetically.

Jessica folded her arms across her chest and looked her twin up and down. "He's picking you up for dinner," Jessica repeated in an accusing tone. "You're a worse boy stealer than Lila!"

Lila gasped indignantly. "I am *not* a boy stealer!"

"Jessica, it wasn't my—" Elizabeth began.

Jessica cut her off. "Don't try to make excuses," she snapped, flouncing back down the hall to her bedroom. "A boy stealer is a boy stealer!"

Lila stormed after Jessica, and before Jessica's door slammed Elizabeth heard the two best friends begin a spirited argument about who had stolen more boys from whom. Elizabeth trudged down the stairs with a sigh. The evening wasn't getting off to a good start.

But the greeting Elizabeth received from Kevin almost made up for the unpleasant scene with Jessica. Kevin jumped out of the Mazda to open the door for her. "Elizabeth, you look beautiful," he declared fervently. "I'm a pretty fortunate guy."

Elizabeth smiled. She enjoyed Kevin's compliments. It had been a while, she realized, since a boy—since Todd—had done or said anything to make her feel special. *Maybe tonight will be fun*, Elizabeth thought optimistically as she slid into the passenger seat.

During the drive downtown, Kevin was as glib and charming a conversationalist as ever. They reached the restaurant and Kevin paused for a moment on the sidewalk. "Is the Box Tree

Café OK with you?" he asked Elizabeth. "Is it absolutely your first choice for dinner tonight? Because I want to take you someplace special. I want this to be a night to remember."

"It's one of the best restaurants in Sweet Valley," Elizabeth assured him.

"A night to remember," Kevin repeated with a satisfied smile when they were seated at one of the café's candlelit outdoor tables. "You don't know what it means to me, Liz, that you agreed to go out with me tonight. You don't know what it does for me."

Kevin's tone struck Elizabeth as odd. *You don't know what it does for me.* If this was flattery, it was a strange sort. Why did she get the feeling that it wasn't just the pleasure of her company Kevin was talking about?

"I never thought it would work out so well," Kevin continued. "Everything's falling into place."

"What's falling into place?" Elizabeth asked, still not sure she knew what Kevin was really trying to express.

Kevin shot her an amused glance over the top of his menu. "My life here in Sweet Valley. It's just the way I wanted it to happen."

"Well, I'm glad you're happy here," she said.

"Happy's not the word for it." Kevin's light eyes glittered with an intensity that didn't seem in keeping with his usual easygoing manner. "Yes, everything's falling into place," he repeated. His hand closed around the knife next to his plate. "It's a good feeling, Elizabeth."

"I'm sure it is," Elizabeth said, watching as Kevin drew the blade of the knife methodically across the table cloth. Her uneasy sense that the conversation was operating on more than one level increased.

Kevin dropped the knife, then reached across the table and touched her hand. "You're just the kind of girl I hoped to meet in California."

Elizabeth moved her hand away from Kevin's on the pretense of closing her menu. "I am?"

"Exactly the kind of girl," Kevin asserted. "Do you have any idea how right we are for each other?"

Elizabeth laughed uncomfortably. If she had thought Kevin was just flirting with her, she'd have been able to go along with it without a problem, but there was a strangely serious undercurrent to everything he said. And his eyes! He was staring at her without blinking. It was distinctly unsettling. "It's a little soon to tell, I'd say," she said lightly.

"I just don't know what you were doing with a guy like Wilkins," Kevin declared. "He can't be your type."

Elizabeth stiffened. Her relationship with Todd was her own business; she certainly had no desire to talk about it with Kevin.

Kevin didn't seem to notice Elizabeth's offended silence. "Todd thought he owned Burlington," Kevin went on, his voice harsh, "and he thought he owned Sweet Valley, but things haven't exactly been going his way lately, have they?"

"I don't know," Elizabeth said guardedly.

"But I don't want to talk about him." Suddenly Kevin's eyes were sparkling and warm again. "Let's talk about you."

In spite of Kevin's professed desire to talk about *her*, they spent most of the dinner talking about *him*. Kevin was clearly his own favorite subject. He talked endlessly about the prospect of working for Mr. Wilkins at Varitronics, and predicted his eventual triumphant return to Burlington.

Elizabeth was glad to let Kevin dominate the conversation. The uncomfortable feeling, once it took root, was hard to shake. At camp, Elizabeth had always found Kevin good company. Now she was surprised to find herself eager for this date to end. *Kevin is incredibly egotistical*, she thought as she spooned into the raspberry sorbet she'd ordered for dessert. And some of his remarks, particularly those about Todd, had been outright nasty, not at all in keeping with her previous impression of Kevin's amiable, generous personality. She couldn't help but recall Todd's hint that maybe Kevin wasn't quite as great a guy as everyone thought.

Kevin paid the check. As they left the café he chatted about what they could do next; meanwhile, Elizabeth searched for an excuse to cut the evening short. "I just remembered something," she said when they reached the Mazda. "I'm supposed to get together with Enid and Aaron tonight so we can prepare a special nature activity with the kids at camp tomorrow. Do you mind taking me home?"

"Sure, I mind, because I'd love to spend more time with you," Kevin replied. "But your wish is my command."

He drove fast; in only a few minutes they pulled up at the curb in front of the Wakefields' house.

"Thanks so much for dinner," Elizabeth said, her hand on the door handle.

Kevin put his own hand on Elizabeth's shoulder, gripping it firmly. "We'll do it again sometime," he insisted.

"Umm," she murmured, not wanting to commit herself.

She expected Kevin to release her. Instead he drew her closer. Before Elizabeth knew what was happening, Kevin's mouth had come down on hers in a hard kiss.

Quickly Elizabeth wriggled from Kevin's grasp. She had no desire to get intimate with him in any way. "Kevin, I really have to go—" Elizabeth broke off. Kevin's face had contorted with anger and frustration. For a split second she was genuinely frightened. Kevin looked as if he might hit her.

But a second later Kevin's expression had metamorphosed once again. He dropped his hands, allowing Elizabeth to jump from the car. Kevin smiled and waved after her, appearing to be the perfect gentleman. "It's been fun, Liz. Thanks. I'll see you tomorrow!"

The Mazda roared off. For a moment Elizabeth stood on the sidewalk and stared after it. She shivered. She wasn't sure what had happened just now, but she knew one thing: She didn't like Kevin nearly as much as she had before their date. There was something about him that wasn't quite right.

Elizabeth felt like crying. Her confusion about Kevin faded and a sharp pang of loneliness took its place. *I miss Todd*, she thought desperately. More than ever, Elizabeth wished she and Todd could sit down and have a long talk.

Without the strong, warm presence of the Todd she used to know, Elizabeth's world seemed empty and a little bit scary.

With an impatient gesture, Todd pointed the remote control and turned off the big-screen TV. He jumped to his feet and resumed pacing. He'd spent the entire evening bouncing from one activity to another. He couldn't be at peace knowing Elizabeth was alone somewhere with Kevin.

Todd heard the door to his father's study down the hall open and close. Mr. Wilkins peered into the recreation room. "I just tried to phone Kevin," he announced, "but he's not in. Would you do me a favor tomorrow at camp and ask him to call me? I have good news. There's definitely a position for him at Varitronics and I want to get him started immediately in the formal application process."

"So you're handing it to him on a silver platter," Todd said bitterly.

Mr. Wilkins frowned. "I'd be happy to do the same for you if you showed half the interest Kevin has shown in Varitronics."

Todd had been on the verge of exploding all evening. Now his pent-up emotions poured out of him like lava from a volcano. "Can I earn your approval only by doing just what you want me to do?" he shouted. "What about what *I* want to do? Like maybe coach? I suppose that doesn't matter. I suppose you'd rather have a son like Kevin!"

Mr. Wilkins's eyebrows shot up in surprise. "Todd, you know that's not true. You're my son and I would never—"

"I don't feel like your son anymore," Todd said hoarsely. "And you don't seem like my dad."

Before his father could respond Todd rushed from the room and from the house.

Todd jumped into his car and turned the ignition key, his hands shaking. He had meant every word he said. He didn't feel close to his father anymore; he couldn't share the most difficult problem he'd ever faced with him. And it was all because of Kevin Holmes.

For half an hour Todd drove aimlessly. Eventually he found himself at Secca Lake. A couple of cars were parked near the lodge, including one with a Fort Carroll High sticker. Todd recognized it as Melissa's. Sometimes a few members of the park staff hung out at the lodge after hours. But Todd wanted to be alone. Hands in his pockets, he strolled toward the water. The park, bathed in soft moonlight, was peaceful. Todd breathed deeply, wishing he could absorb some of the calm.

As he emerged from a group of trees, he realized there was a girl standing on the beach. It was Melissa, apparently enjoying the beauty of the night. As Todd debated whether or not to join her, a shadowy form appeared at her side. Todd heard Melissa cry out; he saw a glint of metal in the moonlight. Someone was attacking her, and he had a knife! Quick as a flash, the man knocked Melissa to the ground and seized her shoulder bag.

Todd had stepped back into the shadows under the trees, overwhelmed by an agonizing sense of déjà vu. It couldn't be, but it was. As the attacker fled across the lawn in the direction of the parking lot Todd got a clear glimpse of the man's face. It was Kevin Holmes.

Todd stood frozen, too stunned and frightened to chase Kevin the way he had that night in Vermont. A moment later he heard the roar of an engine. Todd didn't remember seeing Kevin's Mazda; it must have been parked out of sight at the other end of the lot. Kevin was making his getaway.

Meanwhile, Melissa had jumped to her feet, apparently unharmed. Todd saw her dash into the lodge. He knew there were other people there, and a telephone from which to call the police. Instead of following her into the lodge, Todd trudged back to his car.

He drove slowly out of the parking lot, numb from the battle of conflicting emotions taking place inside him. He'd seen it with his own eyes, just like that time in Burlington. He'd seen Kevin, the real Kevin. *And I let him get away.* Todd's fingers tightened on the steering wheel. *But it's not too late. I can still go after him.* Todd reached an intersection. A right turn would take him into town. He could drive to Kevin's apartment and confront him, force him to turn himself over to the police. If he turned left, he'd be heading away from Kevin's place and in the direction of his own house.

For a long moment, the longest moment of his life, Todd hesitated at the stop sign. Then he stepped on the gas— and turned left.

Todd had never felt so cowardly and low. He knew he'd be haunted forever by the images of Kevin's violence and the knowledge that he'd had the ability to prevent the violence, to save Melissa and the other mugging victims from pain by exposing Kevin, but had chosen not to.

Twelve

Todd lay in bed Thursday morning and stared dully out the window at the rising sun. He hadn't slept a wink the night before. He couldn't relax, even after he had called the twins' phone number and hung up when he heard Elizabeth's voice at the other end of the line. She'd probably gotten home safely from her date well before Todd saw Kevin at Secca Lake.

Elizabeth made it home safely, but Melissa didn't, Todd thought bitterly.

During the hours that he'd lain awake in the dark, horrible images had raced through Todd's consciousness: the glittering knife blade, Kevin hurling Melissa roughly to the ground, Melissa's panicked cry, the cruelty on Kevin's face as he fled the scene of the crime.

Todd dressed slowly. Then, grabbing his gear bag, he slouched down the stairs to the kitchen.

Mr. Wilkins was sitting at the table with *The Wall Street Journal* and a cup of steaming coffee. When his son entered he looked up, a concerned expression on his handsome face. "Have a seat, son," Mr. Wilkins urged. "I'd like for us to talk about what happened last night—"

Todd cut him off. "I don't have time," he said curtly. He grabbed a couple of oranges from the fridge and headed for the door without looking at his father. "Maybe it's not a *real* job." Todd gave the word a bitter, sarcastic emphasis. "But I have to be at the camp anyway. I have a responsibility. Have a good day at the office, Dad." He slammed the door behind him before his father had a chance to respond.

Todd sat for a few minutes in his car before starting the engine. He hoped his father would come after him, insist that Todd explain himself. *I want to tell you, Dad,* Todd thought desperately. *I want to tell you what happened last night. But would you believe me?*

Mr. Wilkins didn't come. Todd started the BMW's engine and drove away.

If he'd known what was waiting for him at Secca Lake, he might have stayed home. A number of cars were already parked in the lot, and side by side were Melissa's and Kevin's. Inside the lodge, Melissa was the center of a concerned group that included Elizabeth and Kevin. Elizabeth glanced quickly at Todd as he entered, then turned her attention back to Melissa.

Sarah Schmidt held one arm supportively around Melissa's shoulders. "Are you sure you want to work today?" she asked. "Maybe you should take it easy and spend a quiet day at home."

Melissa shook her head. "I'm OK," she insisted, although Todd thought she looked a little pale. "I wasn't hurt, just shaken up. I'd rather stay busy. It will keep my mind off things."

"If there's anything we can do to help, all you have to do is ask," Elizabeth told her.

Melissa smiled weakly. "Thanks, Liz. I knew I could count on you guys for support."

"I'm sure you can count on the Sweet Valley police, too," Kevin declared. "I bet they'll have the culprit in no time flat."

Todd watched Kevin's audacious behavior, his perverse boldness. It no longer surprised Todd, but it still sickened him.

"I wasn't able to help the police with a description of the guy, though," Melissa said. "He came up behind me. He was strong and young. That was all I could tell."

"They'll catch him," Kevin predicted. "Don't you worry."

Although he was addressing Melissa, Kevin looked directly at Todd as he spoke. His glance shifted pointedly to Elizabeth, then returned to Todd. *He's flaunting it*, Todd thought, swallowing the accusation that had nearly burst from him. *He doesn't know I witnessed the mugging, but he knows I suspect him—and he knows I'll keep quiet.* Unable to bear the sight of Kevin any longer, Todd turned on his heel and left the lodge.

By the end of camp that day, Todd's nerves were worn to shreds. The sight of Melissa trying to be cheerful as she conducted her usual activities was wrenching and poignant; the sight of Kevin, gloating and hypocritical, was maddening. All day the refrain ran through Todd's brain. *This is wrong, wrong, wrong.*

And the gravest wrong of all, Todd recognized at last, was his own silence and isolation. He'd kept his knowledge of Kevin's criminal character to himself; he'd cut himself off from his friends and family. True, he'd done it in part to protect the people he cared about, but he couldn't hide from the facts any longer. He wasn't protecting anyone by keeping Kevin's secret. On the contrary, he was exposing innocent people to harm.

It was four-thirty; the campers had gone home. As he stuffed half a dozen basketballs into a canvas sack, Todd felt a rush of optimism. He didn't have to wrestle alone with his problem any more. It wasn't too late. He still had friends. They'd help him decide what to do.

As soon as he'd stored the sports equipment, Todd went in search of Aaron and Winston. He found them in the parking lot, about to head to the Dairi Burger in Winston's broken-down orange VW bug.

"Can I come with you guys?" Todd asked urgently.

Winston shot a surprised look at Aaron. "Sure," he said. "Hop in."

Todd wedged himself into the cramped back seat. "I'm glad I caught you," he panted. "I need to talk to you about something important."

"What?" asked Aaron.

"It can wait until we get to the Dairi Burger," Todd said mysteriously. "Just floor it, Egbert."

When the three of them were seated at a relatively secluded booth in the back of the restaurant, Todd took a deep breath. He put his hands on the table and clenched them together to keep them from shaking. "I have to tell you guys about something that happened when I was living in Vermont."

"Go ahead," Winston said after a moment of charged silence.

Todd rapidly recounted the Burlington mugging incident, culminating in Kevin's trial and prison sentence. Next he confessed his recent suspicion of Kevin, a result of the two muggings in downtown Sweet Valley.

"It's not just a suspicion anymore," Todd concluded at last, his eyes glittering feverishly. "I was at the lake last night. I saw Kevin attack Melissa."

As Todd talked, he'd watched astonishment spread over both Winston's and Aaron's faces. Now their expressions clouded with another emotion: disbelief.

"Kevin Holmes, a mugger?" Winston exclaimed.

"If all this is true," Aaron said to Todd, "why didn't you say something sooner? Why didn't you go straight to the police?"

Todd dropped his eyes. He couldn't tell his friends the whole truth. He wasn't ready to admit that Kevin had been capitalizing on his cowardice by blackmailing him; he was too ashamed. "When Kevin first showed up in Sweet Valley, I thought he might have turned over a new leaf," Todd explained. That much at least was true. "My parents knew about him, too, and they believed—they still believe—he's reformed. In fact, my dad's been bending over backward to welcome Kevin to Sweet Valley. He's even getting him a job at Varitronics. My parents' feelings made it harder to accept that Kevin could still be a criminal. I just didn't want to believe it. I didn't want to deal with it."

"But if you saw Kevin last night," Winston pressed, "why didn't you turn him into the police?"

Todd shook his head. "I just couldn't," he said lamely, wishing he could explain that he'd still been afraid for Elizabeth's sake. "But I'm going to. Today, or tomorrow. I'm ready now.

You've got to promise you won't tell anybody what I've told you. Not until I've had a chance to talk to the police."

Winston and Aaron looked at one another and nodded. "Sure," Winston agreed.

Enormously relieved, Todd let out a big sigh. "Thanks, you guys. Thanks for helping me out."

"Sure, Todd," Aaron said cautiously. "Anytime."

Winston and Aaron ordered some food, but Todd couldn't eat. He left his friends and took a bus back to Secca Lake to retrieve his car. Driving home, he opened all the car windows and let the Pacific breeze rake through his hair. For the first time in two weeks Todd felt clean and whole. Until that day he hadn't fully realized that by keeping silent he had seriously undermined his own dignity and self-esteem.

The discovery set Todd free. He knew what he had to do. *It's time to take charge of my life again*, Todd determined fiercely. *Kevin is the one who should be cowering, not me!*

Todd spent Thursday night working things out in his head, and spying on Kevin Holmes. His conversation that afternoon with Aaron and Winston had boosted Todd's confidence, but he wanted to be one hundred percent sure of himself before he took his story to the police. He did not, however, intend to let Kevin commit another crime. So he parked his car in the shadows half a block from Kevin's apartment. Todd was prepared to follow Kevin, even confront him, but Kevin never left his apartment. Finally, close to dawn, Todd drove home.

He managed to catch an hour of sleep before he started out on Friday morning. His plan was to stop at Secca Lake and tell Mr. Schiavitti that, even though it was the last day of camp, he needed to be excused from counselor duties for part of the morning. Then he would head to the Sweet Valley police station.

As Todd pulled into the Secca Lake parking lot, he was startled by the sight that met his bloodshot eyes. Two police squad cars were parked by the lodge. *They caught him,* Todd thought exultantly. The police hadn't required his help after all. They'd caught Kevin! Todd parked the BMW and sprinted toward the lodge. He wanted to see what was going on. He wanted to be in on Kevin's arrest.

He burst through the door of the lodge. Inside, four police officers were talking with Mr. Schiavitti and Sarah. Standing off to the side were a number of the camp counselors: Elizabeth, Jessica, Enid, Aaron, and Kyle, their eyes wide with shock and dismay. And Kevin was present, too.

But something was wrong. Todd stopped in his tracks. Kevin wasn't in handcuffs. Kevin wasn't even the object of the police officers' attention. Kevin was smiling.

"Are you Todd Wilkins?" one of the officers asked in a businesslike voice.

"Yes," Todd answered.

"Todd, we'd like to ask you to come down to the station with us. We'd like to question you about the assault of Melissa Milliken two nights ago."

Todd, stunned and exhausted, felt the room begin to spin around him. As the police escorted him from the lodge, he could focus on only two things: the tears in Elizabeth's eyes and Kevin's triumphant smile.

Todd rode in the back seat of one of the squad cars. The officers did not speak to him until they were inside the station. Then one of the officers led him into a small conference room. Seated at one end of a rectangular table was Melissa.

"Is this your pen?"

Todd snapped out of his daze. Officer Elliott, one of the two officers seated at the table, was holding something out to him.

Todd took the pen. The initials "TPW" were engraved on it. "Yes, it's mine," Todd said. "It was a gift from my father. But I keep it in the glove compartment of my car. How did you—"

"It was found by one of our investigators yesterday on the beach at Secca Lake. At the precise location of the crime that took place two nights ago," Officer Elliott added significantly.

"It couldn't have been," Todd exclaimed. "I

173

wasn't carrying the pen, it was in my car, and I didn't go on the beach, I stayed on the grass—''

Todd stopped. The color drained from his face as he realized how incriminating his words must have sounded.

The officer turned to Melissa. "Melissa, did you see Todd at Secca Lake the night you were assaulted?"

Melissa addressed Officer Elliott. "No, I didn't see Todd," she replied carefully. "I didn't really see anyone."

"Let me rephrase the question," said Officer Elliott. "Do you know who attacked you?"

"I'm not sure." Melissa shivered. "I didn't see the man's—the boy's—face. It was dark, and he came up behind me, and it happened so quickly. But he was tall, and when he told me to give him my bag or else, his voice sounded young. It sounded familiar."

"Might it have been the voice of someone you work with at the day camp?" Officer Elliott suggested.

Todd sat on the edge of his chair and stared at Melissa. Without looking at him, she nodded. "I couldn't place it at the time, but yes, it might have been."

Todd was still clutching the pen. Now he dropped it on the table with a clatter. "But, Melissa," he croaked. "Melissa, it wasn't me. You know it wasn't me. It was—" Todd's voice failed him. She wouldn't believe him and Officer Elliott wouldn't believe him; no one would believe him now.

"I'm sorry, Todd, but on this basis of this evidence we're going to have to detain you for further questioning," Officer Elliott announced dispassionately. "I'm going to read you your rights and then you'll be free to phone your parents and arrange for legal counsel."

Melissa and the other policeman left the room, leaving Todd and Officer Elliott alone.

This can't be happening. Todd slumped in his chair. *I must be dreaming, a bad dream.* He was dreaming that Kevin stole the pen from his glove compartment and planted it on the beach to make it look as if Todd had mugged Melissa. He was dreaming that Kevin had framed him for the crime. *It's all a bad dream. It has to be. It can't be real.*

But it was real. Officer Elliott was reading Todd his rights.

Suddenly Todd saw the light. Kevin had done his time in jail and now Todd was going to do his. This, at last, was Kevin's revenge.

Thirteen

The Secca Lake day camp was in an uproar. Though the counselors were conducting activities as usual, Todd's arrest was all any of them could think or talk about.

Elizabeth had been glad to get away from the other counselors, to disappear into the woods for a nature walk with the Sandpiper cluster. She needed to be alone. She couldn't bear even Enid's company; Elizabeth had left her friend and Aaron and the rest of the nature group far behind.

But even in the woods, Elizabeth couldn't hide from the memory of Todd's face when he'd entered the lodge a few hours earlier to find the police waiting for him. *Todd*, Elizabeth thought hopelessly as she watched the campers swarm over a fallen tree trunk they were pretending was a fort. *Todd, could you really have done such a thing?*

She looked at her watch with a sigh. It was time to head back to the lodge for lunch. She was dreading it; she knew what would be going on there.

Everyone was discussing the charges against Todd. "We just got word from the police station," Elizabeth overheard Winston say to Aaron as she came in, "and they've put Todd under formal arrest."

Elizabeth stopped in the entrance to the lodge, her hand gripping the door. She felt as if she were going to be sick.

Jessica and Enid both bolted to Elizabeth's side. "Come over here, Liz," Jessica said. She put an arm around her twin and practically carried her to one of the benches along the wall of the lodge.

In her concern for Elizabeth, Jessica had completely forgotten her resentment over her sister's date with Kevin. "Have a sandwich, Liz," Jessica urged. "You'll feel better if you eat something."

To make her sister happy, Elizabeth took the sandwich, but she couldn't eat it.

"Maybe you should go home," Enid suggested. "I'm sure Mr. Schiavitti would understand."

Elizabeth shook her head. "I'm fine," she insisted. "I just need to think."

Enid, Jessica, and Cara fell respectfully silent.

Their silence forced Elizabeth to listen to the other counselors' conversation.

Winston, Aaron, Kevin, Jill, Kyle, and Ed were sitting in a huddle. "Do you really think he did it?" Jill asked. "Do you believe Todd could have robbed Melissa?"

"I believe it," Ed declared. "He's been a bully from day one."

Elizabeth stiffened. Enid patted her arm. "He's just upset," Enid whispered. "Don't forget, he's a friend of Melissa's from school. He doesn't mean it."

But Ed did mean it. And he wasn't the only one who was prepared to bet on Todd's guilt. "The police must have some pretty hard evidence," Kyle said in a case-closed tone.

"They don't arrest people without a reason. And you remember what I told you about the kind of thing Todd was up to in Vermont," Kevin said meaningfully.

Elizabeth lifted her eyes. Kevin was in profile so she couldn't see the expression on his face very well. But for a moment she thought he was smiling.

She waited for Aaron and Winston to speak up for Todd. Instead they simply nodded in response to Kevin's remark. Elizabeth turned back to Jessica, Cara, and Enid, her eyes seeking an explanation of Kevin's mysterious words. Enid looked as puzzled as Elizabeth herself. Jessica and Cara exchanged a quick glance, then shrugged in unison.

Isn't anybody going to say anything? Elizabeth wondered. *Doesn't anyone believe in Todd?*

"Let's go outside," Jessica said. "It's time to start afternoon activities."

Kevin, Jill, Kyle, and Ed had just headed out as well. Elizabeth followed Enid, Jessica, and Cara to the door of the lodge. Only Aaron and Winston remained seated. Behind her, Elizabeth heard Aaron clear his throat. *He's going to defend Todd*, she thought with a rush of gratitude. Hungry to overhear some hopeful words, she paused in the doorway, out of Winston and Aaron's line of vision.

"Todd admitted he was at the lake the other night," Aaron said to Winston in a low, shaky voice. "What if he said that about—what if he made up that other story to cover for something he did himself?"

Winston didn't answer Aaron's question directly. "He's been acting so strangely lately," Winston commented. "And yesterday at the Dairi Burger he had me worried. I don't know, Dallas. I'm afraid it could be true."

No, it couldn't! Elizabeth wanted to scream.

Half blind with tears, Elizabeth hurried from the lodge and toward the lake, eager to escape the dark shadow of Aaron and Winston's disloyalty. The sunlit water was a bright blur to her eyes but as she stared fixedly at it, one thing became crystal-clear to

Elizabeth. Todd was innocent. Elizabeth felt it, in the depths of her soul. Todd could never hurt another person. He might have grown moody and unpredictable, he might have stopped loving her, but Elizabeth knew that no matter how much Todd might have changed on the surface, how idiosyncratic his behavior might have become, the integrity of his character was unshakable.

"Todd is innocent," Elizabeth declared to the seagulls flocked at the water's edge. She knew it beyond a shadow of a doubt; and as soon as she got home she would get advice from her father about Todd's legal predicament. Elizabeth was ready to do absolutely everything in her power to get Todd free.

"This barbecue is a bomb," Cara said to Jessica with a depressed sigh.

The barbecue was being held to celebrate the last day of camp. The children were having a blast, but the counselors were somber, thinking about Melissa's mugging and Todd's arrest.

"Tell me about it." Jessica looked toward Elizabeth, who was sitting alone on the fringes of the party. "This is the worst thing that's ever happened to me."

"The worst thing that's ever happened to *you*?" Cara repeated. "How about being the worst thing that's ever happened to Melissa and Todd and Elizabeth?"

"Everything that hurts Liz hurts me, too," Jessica said quietly.

"I know." Cara sighed again. "But maybe we should try to look on the bright side. Maybe the police made a mistake."

"I wish," Jessica said. "But it all makes sense. It fits with what Kevin told us about Todd the other day."

"I guess we never knew the real Todd Wilkins," Cara concluded. "It's so sad."

Jessica watched as Kevin approached the two girls, juggling three plates of food. He was smiling, his light green eyes glittering like emeralds.

"What are you so cheerful about?" Jessica asked him as she took one of the plates.

"There's a silver lining to every cloud," Kevin told her, an exultant note in his voice. "You just need to know where to look for it."

Cara took her plate, then put it down. "I can't eat," she said.

Jessica frowned down at her own plate. The hamburger and salad didn't look at all appetizing. "Let's get some kind of game started," she suggested. "That might distract us."

"We need some mindless fun," Cara agreed. "How about team Frisbee?"

"There's a Frisbee in my car," Kevin told them. "On the back seat, I think. It's not locked."

"I'll go get it." Jessica proposed. "Be right back."

She ran to the parking lot, glad to have something concrete to do. Kevin's car was parked at the far end of the lot. "I can't believe he doesn't lock it," Jessica panted as she leaned into the back of the Mazda. After the recent muggings, people had started to take some precautions. "He's lucky someone doesn't rip him off."

As Jessica grabbed the Frisbee she spotted something sparkling on the floor of the car, half under the seat. She reached for it. It was a gold lavaliere! *My necklace. I almost lost it!* Jessica thought, putting a hand to her throat.

But her necklace was still in place. This was the twin to Jessica's gold lavaliere. It was Elizabeth's.

Jessica straightened up and tried to remember when Elizabeth had lost her necklace. It must have been when she had her date with Kevin, Jessica speculated. No, that wasn't right. Jessica couldn't recall the exact day Elizabeth's lavaliere had disappeared, but she was certain it was well before the night Kevin and Elizabeth had gone out to dinner. Which meant . . .

What *did* it mean? If Elizabeth hadn't lost the necklace when she was out with Kevin, how had it come to be under the seat of Kevin's car?

A new consideration struck Jessica. Elizabeth wasn't the only person who'd lost something recently. Now that she thought about it, she realized there'd been a lot of mysterious disappearances. Cara's keychain, Ed's watch, Winston's baseball cap. Were the disappearances

ances related? Jessica stared at the lavaliere in her hand. Then she closed her eyes and pictured Kevin—handsome, wonderful Kevin. Could Kevin be a petty thief?

Jessica didn't know what to think. She tucked the lavaliere in the pocket of her shorts and slammed the door of the Mazda. Frisbee in hand, she hurried back to the barbecue. She scanned the lawn rapidly. Kevin was nowhere in sight, and neither was Elizabeth.

"Psst! Cara!" Jessica hissed. "Enid!" Cara and Enid looked startled to see Jessica beckoning at them from behind the trunk of a tree. "Get Aaron and Winston, and get over here!" Jessica commanded.

A few seconds later, the five were huddled behind the tree. "Look," Jessica said as she pulled the lavaliere from her pocket. "It's the necklace Elizabeth lost last week. You'll never guess where I found it!"

"But how could it have been in Kevin's car?" Cara exclaimed after Jessica told them about her discovery in the parking lot.

"All I know is, it was there," Jessica confirmed.

"Do you mean to say you think Elizabeth didn't lose the necklace after all, but that Kevin *stole* it?" Winston asked, befuddled.

Jessica nodded "It looks like it. And if he stole this, then maybe he stole some other things, too."

"My keys!" Cara cried.

"My lucky baseball cap!" Winston yelped.

Jessica couldn't help but giggle. "That's right. Although I don't know why anyone would want to steal your dumb hat."

"It's not a dumb hat," Winston protested. "It's—"

"Shut up, Egbert," Aaron snapped. "Get serious. Don't you see what this means?"

Winston stared blankly at Aaron. Then his eyes lit up with comprehension. "What Todd told us about Kevin," Winston gasped. "It was true."

"What are you talking about?" Jessica demanded. "What did Todd tell you?"

"Yesterday, the day after Melissa was mugged," Aaron explained. "He told us he *did* know Kevin in Vermont. And he said that Kevin had been arrested for mugging an old man in downtown Burlington."

"Kevin would have gotten away with the crime if Todd hadn't caught him red-handed," Winston contributed.

"But that's not all," Aaron added. "Todd said he was at Secca Lake on Wednesday night. He'd had an argument with his father and he went for a drive." Aaron paused significantly. "He said he saw the person who attacked Melissa."

Jessica's spine tingled. "Who was it?" she asked.

"According to Todd, it was Kevin."

Cara gasped.

"Kevin!" Enid cried. "But if Kevin attacked Melissa, why did the police arrest Todd?"

"Good question," Winston said.

"This is so confusing," Jessica burst out in frustration. "Todd's story about Kevin in Vermont, Kevin's story about Todd—who do we believe?"

Her question was greeted by a baffled silence. "Yesterday we thought Todd was lying," Aaron said slowly. "But now, since you found the necklace, maybe . . ."

"Maybe Todd was telling the truth," Winston finished.

"Then maybe," Jessica concluded in a shaky voice, "the wrong person is behind bars!"

Fourteen

"I came as soon as I heard," Mr. Wilkins told Todd as he strode into the station. "I was out of town for a meeting or I would have been here sooner. Are you all right, son?"

Todd had been keeping his emotions under strict control all day. But the love and concern on his father's face brought tears to his eyes. He cleared his throat twice before he answered. "I'm fine, Dad. I haven't spoken with Mom yet, though. She was going to L.A. for the day to shop."

"Don't worry. We'll get home before she does," Mr. Wilkins said.

"Can I really go home?" Todd asked eagerly.

"Because you're a minor, you're free on my recognizance until the hearing," Mr. Wilkins confirmed. "Come on. Let's go home and talk this over."

On the sidewalk outside the police station, Todd stopped and took a deep breath of fresh air. He'd never valued his freedom so much until he'd come close to losing it. *And it's not over yet*, Todd reminded himself. *I know the truth, but no one else does. No one but Kevin.*

If there was one thing the hours in the police station had taught him, it was that the freedom he'd always taken for granted was linked to a responsibility, a responsibility he'd been shirking.

Todd and his father climbed into Mr. Wilkins's Mercedes. As Mr. Wilkins started the engine, Todd realized that for the first time in a long while, he and his father were actually talking civilly to one another. In the crisis, they'd forgotten to fight.

"I didn't do it, Dad," Todd said simply.

"I know it, son," Mr. Wilkins replied. "But you still have some explaining to do. How did you get involved in a situation like this?"

It was a long story and Todd wasn't sure where to begin. "I'm involved because of . . . because of Kevin," he said at last.

"Because of Kevin?"

Todd knew the best thing to do was tell the truth, plain and simple. "Kevin framed me," he explained. "Last week, when someone broke the windows on my car, well, I knew it was Kevin. The glove compartment was open, too, but at the time I didn't notice anything missing. But now I know he stole the pen from the glove compartment and planted it so it would look as if I were the one who jumped Melissa. I did actually witness the mugging Dad. I drove out to Secca Lake that night, after you and I . . . and I saw it. Kevin was the one who attacked Melissa."

Mr. Wilkins drew in a deep breath. For a long moment he didn't respond to Todd's startling announcement. His heart pounding in his chest, Todd waited tensely for his father's judgment. Finally he couldn't bear it any longer. He had to know. "Do you believe me, Dad?" Todd asked in a hoarse whisper.

Mr. Wilkins didn't hesitate. "Of course I believe you. You've never lied to me, Todd. I know you, and I trust you."

No words had ever meant more to Todd. It was as if an immeasurable weight had been lifted from his shoulders. His father believed in him. *And I believe in myself again*, Todd realized. It had been a while since he'd felt so strong. He wasn't going to hide anymore, from himself or from his responsibilities.

"I know you're shocked about Kevin, and probably disappointed, too," Todd said.

"Shocked and disappointed. Yes," Mr. Wilkins admitted. "I am. And I'm puzzled. There are still a lot of things I don't understand. But my prime concern right now is your legal situation. We'll get all this straightened out," he promised his son.

Todd nodded. He knew they would. With his father standing by him, he could do anything.

Suddenly Todd was struck by an unexpected contrast. He remembered when Kevin had been in trouble in Vermont. Yes, Kevin had been guilty of the mugging and Mr. Holmes had been willing to bribe Todd not to testify against Kevin, but neither of Kevin's parents had put in an appearance at the trial. Kevin had faced the ordeal all alone.

I'm lucky, Todd thought. He knew that no matter how serious a mistake he might make, his parents would always do their best to understand him and to support him.

Mr. Wilkins broke into his son's reverie. "We have a lot to talk about, Todd."

"I know, Dad," Todd replied. "I want to tell you everything that's happened since Kevin arrived in Sweet Valley." *And some things from before that.* Todd thought again of the bribe. "But first can you drive me to Secca Lake? I just have to . . . pick up my car. It's in the parking lot. Then I'll meet you at home and we can talk."

"Sure thing, son."

There was a lot Todd wanted to say to his father. But there was one other conversation that was even more urgent. It was time for a confrontation with Kevin.

Elizabeth looked on dully as the Sandpiper and Eagle clusters held a watermelon-seed-spitting contest. After two weeks of working with the campers and the other counselors, she felt very close to all of them. She knew she should play with the kids, try to get into the spirit of the last-day celebration, but she couldn't. She couldn't stop thinking about Todd. Elizabeth was sure he was innocent, but also sure that he was in very deep trouble. For a while she'd felt better having determined she would do all she could to help him. But now old fears crept back into Elizabeth's heart. What if Todd just pushed her away again? What if this crisis only made the distance between the two of them harder to bridge?

Just another half an hour and then I can get out of here, Elizabeth thought.

"Liz, why don't you join the contest?"

Elizabeth raised her eyes. Kevin stood in front of her, holding out a juicy slice of watermelon. She mustered a weak smile. "Watermelon-seed spitting was never my best sport."

"You seem distracted," he observed, his manner sympathetic.

"I am," Elizabeth admitted.

"I understand," Kevin assured her. "Tell you

191

what, let's take a walk. If you want to talk I'll be happy to listen, and if you don't, that's fine, too."

Elizabeth had no intention of confiding in Kevin about something this personal, but she was relieved not to have to think about her relationship—or non-relationship—with Todd for a few minutes. *A walk might help clear my mind*, she thought. "That would be great, she said."

They crossed the lawn together and headed for the nature trail that wound through the woods alongside the lake. Distracted by her own troubles, Elizabeth was hardly aware of Kevin's presence at her side. He remained silent, apparently in tune with her solitary mood.

As soon as they were under the trees and out of sight of the camp barbecue, Kevin's manner changed. His step quickened and he began to talk, his voice harsh and loud. "You shouldn't waste your time being upset about Wilkins," Kevin declared. "He's getting what he deserves."

Elizabeth was jolted out of her preoccupation. She turned to Kevin with a startled expression. "What do you mean, he's getting what he deserves? How can you say that? We don't really know what happened!"

Kevin smiled at her, his light eyes glittering. "*I* know what happened. It happened just as I expected it would. Todd thought he was untouchable, above it all. He thought he could never make a mistake." Kevin's laugh was hard, sardonic, triumphant.

Elizabeth felt a little nervous. She remembered their dinner date earlier that week and how uncomfortable she had been with Kevin. She had managed to avoid him since then; this was the first time they'd been alone together. *Why did I come with him now?* she thought.

"You still want to defend him, don't you?" Kevin guessed. "Well, you're the only one. Everyone else has seen what Todd is really like."

Elizabeth felt dizzy, as if someone had spun her in circles. What was Kevin talking about?

"How could you know what happened the other night?" she asked him. "How can you be so sure?"

"Todd's guilty!" Kevin yelled, a manic gleam in his eyes. "Get that through your head, Liz. All I did was make sure he got what was coming to him."

Elizabeth was more than nervous now; she was scared. She'd never seen Kevin like this, not even on that dinner date. He'd turned into a frightening stranger. And he *was* a stranger, she realized. To her, and to all of them. They'd only been acquainted, and in the most superficial way, for two weeks. What did any of them really know about Kevin Holmes?

The woods were dim. *How far have we walked?* Elizabeth wondered, her panic rising. *If I scream, will anyone hear me?*

*   *   *

"Thanks, Dad," Todd said as he hopped out of his father's car in the Secca Lake parking lot. "I'll be home soon."

Todd watched his father drive off, then sprinted toward the gathering of campers and counselors on the wide lawn. He scanned the crowd, searching for Kevin.

But first Todd spotted Jessica, Enid, Cara, Winston, and Aaron standing in a tight bundle. Todd strode quickly in their direction. "Where's Kevin?" he demanded.

Todd's Sweet Valley High friends jumped at the sound of his voice. "Todd!" Jessica squealed, clutching Kevin's Frisbee to her chest.

"Where'd you come from?" Winston yelped.

"Never mind me, where's Kevin?" Todd repeated urgently.

"We were just wondering that," said Aaron. "We think we've found out—"

"That he's a thief," Cara put in. "Maybe worse."

"And we want to get the real story from him," Aaron concluded.

"He was here just a minute ago," Cara pointed out. "He can't have gone far."

Kevin's gone. Todd looked around him. Kevin had to be at the barbecue somewhere. But where?

Jessica, who'd also been searching the grounds

with her eyes, let out a cry of dismay. "You guys, Liz is gone, too!"

The blood drained from Todd's face. Kevin's threats echoed madly in Todd's brain. *No*, he thought. *No*. Todd ran toward the crowd of campers and counselors. "Where's Kevin? Where's Elizabeth? Has anyone seen them?" he called desperately.

Kyle, who was playing badminton at the edge of the lawn, answered, "I saw them go into the woods just a few minutes ago. They took the nature trail."

A wave of dread pinned Todd to the spot. *Just a few minutes ago*. Was he too late? Had his worst fears already been realized?

"I have to get back now." Though Elizabeth tried to keep her voice calm and unconcerned, it trembled.

Kevin seemed to detect her fear. Infuriated, he grabbed her arm. His grip was hard and bruising.

Elizabeth gasped in pain. "Let me go!" she cried.

Kevin tightened his grip, making escape impossible. "Why are you scared of me, Liz?" he demanded.

"I—I'm not scared of you," Elizabeth lied. "I just want to go."

"You don't need to be scared of me," Kevin continued as if he hadn't even heard her response. "I'm not a criminal. I never meant to hurt anybody." The words rapped out mechanically. "The car accident—I was driving—but it was an accident. I didn't want him to die. He was my brother. I never meant to hurt him." Kevin was holding both of Elizabeth's arms now. As he spoke he pressed her back against the trunk of a tree. "Todd thinks I want to hurt people, but I don't. I really don't."

A car accident? A brother? Suddenly Elizabeth recalled that while Kevin had told her he was an only child, Jessica had heard a different story. Elizabeth had never followed up on the contradiction, assuming Jessica had simply made a mistake. Now she wondered what kind of family secret Kevin Holmes was hiding. And these vehement, bitter accusations against Todd—what was behind *them*?

But the details didn't matter. What mattered right now was that Kevin Holmes was mentally unstable and violent, and he was about to snap—Elizabeth could feel it.

Keep him calm. Keep him talking.

"I'm sorry about the accident," Elizabeth said. Her body was shaking, but she managed to keep her voice low and even. "But what does all of this have to do with Todd? What do you want with him? What do you want with me?"

Kevin answered slowly. It was as if he was putting his jumbled, disconnected thoughts together for the first time. "I want Todd to know what it's like to be in jail," he said. "I want him to know what it feels like to be deserted by everybody he cares about—by his parents, by you. I want him to know what it feels like to have everyone lose faith in him. The same way they did when—"

Kevin broke off his strange speech. His gaze refocused on Elizabeth's terrified face. The pale green eyes gleamed with murderous intent. "I wanted to hurt Todd," Kevin hissed. His hands slid up Elizabeth's arms to her neck. "I have hurt him. But it wasn't enough. I've got one way left to hurt him now."

Kevin's fingers tightened around her throat. Elizabeth felt her breath being cut off. She opened her mouth to scream, but no sound emerged. Kevin squeezed harder.

Then, just as Elizabeth began to grow weak and dizzy, she heard a crash in the underbrush. With a shout Todd leapt out from the trees. He seized Kevin's shoulders, pulled him from Elizabeth, and hurled him down. Winston and Aaron, who were right behind Todd, pinned Kevin to the ground.

Elizabeth stumbled forward and her knees buckled. Before she could fall, Todd caught her and enveloped her in a strong embrace.

"You're safe," he whispered. "I've got you. And I'm never going to let you go again."

Fifteen

Kevin was being questioned by Officer Elliott at the Sweet Valley police station. He sat with his shoulders slumped. His eyes were dull. Todd, Mr. Wilkins, and Elizabeth stood on the other side of the room.

Todd held one arm firmly around Elizabeth and she rested her head against his shoulder. Every now and then she shuddered. Todd, too, hadn't fully recovered his composure. He knew it would be a long time before he forgot seeing Kevin with his hands at Elizabeth's throat. *If I'd arrived one minute later . . .* Todd squeezed his eyes shut. He couldn't even bear to think about it.

"Do you want to tell us what happened at the park just now?" Officer Elliott prompted Kevin.

"I—I'm not sure what happened," Kevin

said, his voice broken and pathetic. "I guess I lost—I lost my temper. I'm sorry, Liz."

Todd felt Elizabeth tense. He held her even closer to his side.

"Have you lost your temper like that before?" asked Officer Elliott.

"I know what you're asking. It was me the other night by the lake," Kevin admitted. "I saw Melissa walking by the water and I just wanted—I just wanted to take something from her. And the old man, and the lady, I just had to take something from them. I never meant to hurt anybody."

The man in Vermont, too, Todd thought. But why? Why would Kevin, who seemed to have so much, need to take from others?

Kevin looked across the room at Todd. For once Kevin's gaze wasn't cruel and intimidating. His expression struck Todd as that of a very young, very sad man.

Officer Elliott asked the question that was hanging in the stuffy air of the station.

"Why? Why did you want to take things?"

"I had a brother," Kevin began. "Brent. He was two years older than me. My big brother." His eyes slid from Todd to Mr. Wilkins. "He was my father's favorite," Kevin continued. "He looked a lot like my father, and he was smart like him. He was supposed to inherit my father's business. That's what Dad wanted, and Brent wanted it, too."

For a moment Kevin's gaze lost its focus.

Todd couldn't be sure, but it looked as if Kevin was crying. Then Kevin smiled crookedly. "Brent was a great brother. I wanted to be just like him. I tried so hard."

Kevin looked again at Todd. Todd found himself nodding, as if to show Kevin he understood. "I studied like mad to get A's and I played three varsity sports. But Brent was still my father's favorite. It wasn't that I thought I could take his place—I knew that was impossible. I just wanted to share." His voice dropped almost to a whisper. "Maybe there just wasn't room for me. Maybe Dad only had room in his heart for one son."

Todd glanced at his father. Mr. Wilkins's expression was stern but compassionate.

After a moment's silence Kevin resumed speaking. "It was two years ago. I was sixteen. I'd just gotten my learner's permit and Brent was teaching me how to drive. He was a great big brother."

Todd heard Elizabeth sniffle. He looked down at her and saw that she had tears in her eyes.

"He let me take the wheel," Kevin continued. "He probably shouldn't have; it was a steep, twisty mountain road. I don't know how it happened. I didn't see the sign warning about the curve. The car spun out of control. I woke up in the hospital. My injuries were nothing—scratches and bruises, a broken arm. But Brent . . ." Kevin's voice cracked. "Brent didn't need the hospital. Brent died instantly."

Elizabeth had buried her face in her hands. Todd wrapped both his arms around her in a comforting hug. His eyes never left Kevin's face.

Kevin looked pleadingly at Mr. Wilkins. "You see, don't you?" he pleaded. "It was an accident. I loved my brother. But my parents, especially my father, they blamed me for it. Nothing could ever make up to them for Brent's loss. I tried. I can't tell you how hard I tried. But it was never enough. Once . . . once my father told me he wished *I'd* died in the crash instead of Brent."

Elizabeth gasped in horror and Mr. Wilkins shook his head. Todd tried to imagine what hearing that must have been like for Kevin. How would *he* have felt if his father had said something so cruel to him?

The pieces of the puzzle were falling into place. *Kevin couldn't do anything right, so he decided to do everything wrong,* Todd guessed. Most likely the robbery in Burlington was a desperate attempt to get his father's attention; perhaps inevitably, it backfired. Mr. Holmes might have been willing to bribe Todd to keep Kevin out of jail, but that didn't mean his opinion of his only surviving son hadn't sunk even lower than before. Todd bet Mr. Holmes couldn't wait to get Kevin out of Burlington.

"I had a lot of time to think in jail," Kevin said flatly. "I thought about you."

Todd started. Kevin was addressing him

now, and the look of sorrow had been replaced by one of poisonous resentment and envy. "You had it all, Wilkins. That was the impression I got during the trial and when I got to Sweet Valley I found out it was true. So why were you out to get me?"

"I wasn't out to get you," Todd said simply. "I was only trying to do the right thing."

"And it was easy for you," Kevin said bitterly. "Doing the right thing. I've never been able to do the right thing, no matter how hard I tried." His eyes grew dreamy. "But then I came out to California and I saw how it could be. *You* were the son who was having a hard time pleasing his father. *I* was going to get a job at Varitronics. Everything was going to work out fine."

Kevin's plot for revenge began to make a twisted sort of sense to Todd. Kevin had made Todd into an alter ego. Unable to please his own parents, Kevin had tried to sabotage Todd's relationship with his father and sought approval from Mr. Wilkins for himself. He'd shifted the blame for his problem onto Todd and then tried to destroy him.

He tried to turn me into him and himself into me, Todd thought.

"Everything was working out," Kevin repeated dully. "It was *my* turn."

"But then you started to lose your temper, to take things," Officer Elliott observed quietly.

"It seemed like everyone had more than I

did. Everyone had something precious," Kevin responded. "Everyone had something I wanted. Like the necklaces Elizabeth and Jessica wear, the necklaces that prove how much their parents love them."

"You took my necklace!" Elizabeth burst out.

Kevin nodded. "But taking things wasn't enough. Even if Todd had gone to jail, that wouldn't have been enough. Nothing would have been enough." Kevin's voice had faded to a whisper and his head dropped onto his folded arms.

Todd knew what Kevin was saying. Kevin had been driven over the edge by the realization that no matter how much he stole, how badly he wounded other people, his own wound wouldn't heal.

The confession was over. For Todd, there was total vindication—his name was cleared—but no joy. *Kevin was right about one thing*, he thought. *When he said he and I aren't that different, he was right*. Kevin was deeply troubled, but at bottom all he wanted was to be accepted and liked, to do the right thing.

Now he's Kevin again and I'm Todd. And Todd had a feeling that for Kevin, that would be the harshest punishment of all.

Half an hour later Todd and Mr. Wilkins were driving home alone. At last it was time to talk things over. Todd told his father about the events of the preceding weeks; the threats that revealed Kevin's reformation as a charade, Kevin's antagonism on the basketball court and elsewhere, his broad hints—always to Todd alone—that he was responsible for the two muggings that preceded the attack on Melissa. Todd even told his father about Mr. Holmes having offered Todd money not to testify against Kevin.

"I wish you'd told me about all of this sooner," Mr. Wilkins said when Todd finished his account. "It was too much for you to deal with on your own. But I understand what you were trying to do. I'm sorry, son. I'm sorry I didn't take your warnings about Kevin seriously."

"It's OK, Dad," Todd hurried to assure him. "You were just giving Kevin the benefit of the doubt."

"No, it was more than that," Mr. Wilkins said. "Let me admit it, Todd. I was flattered by Kevin's interest in Varitronics. It was the sort of enthusiasm I'd always hoped to see from you."

Todd was moved by his father's honesty. He responded with honesty of his own. "I knew it, Dad. And it made me mad. It didn't seem fair."

"It wasn't fair," Mr. Wilkins conceded. "I guess I thought that you just needed a push in the direction of business. Fostering some harmless competition between you and Kevin looked like a way to give you that push."

"I have to choose my own path, Dad," Todd said quietly.

Mr. Wilkins glanced at his son. "I know that now. I know I have to let you determine your own life." He smiled wryly. "But you have to understand it's hard for a parent. It's hard to accept that your child isn't a child anymore."

"I still need your advice, Dad," Todd said.

"But you're growing up. You know what, Todd? I know I can trust you to make good choices based on solid values. I'm proud of you."

Todd turned away from his father, his eyes directed unseeingly out the car window. *He's proud of me, he says. Well, I'm not very proud of myself.*

"It's a tragedy," Mr. Wilkins mused.

"All that time Kevin was only trying to make his father listen, but his father couldn't," Todd commented.

"Couldn't, or wouldn't," Mr. Wilkins added. "I made the same mistake, Todd. If I'd listened to *you*, valued you for what you are instead of expecting you to be someone you're not, maybe none of this would have happened."

"It's not your fault, Dad," Todd insisted. "I'm the one who knew early on that Kevin hadn't really reformed. I should have stood up to him sooner; I could have saved the mugging victims from their pain. I was a coward, Dad. I didn't take action sooner because Kevin intimidated me. I thought if I kept quiet, he wouldn't carry out his threat against Liz."

Todd hung his head, overcome by guilt and shame.

Without taking his eyes off the road, Mr. Wilkins put a hand on his son's shoulder. "Don't be too hard on yourself," he said. "You had courage when it counted. After all, you saved Elizabeth before she could become Kevin's next victim."

Todd knew this was true. He had learned a lesson. He'd never let anyone threaten him into compromising himself again. And he had a feeling that because he had learned this lesson the hard way, he had learned it particularly well.

Sixteen

"I'm OK, really," Elizabeth assured Steven.

The entire Wakefield family was sitting in the living room. Surrounded by her parents and sister and brother, Elizabeth felt safe. It was hard to believe that only a few hours earlier she'd been alone in the woods at Secca Lake with Kevin, her life hanging by a thread.

Steven was holding Elizabeth's hand. He felt her shiver and squeezed her hand supportively.

"I'm OK because Todd got there just in time," Elizabeth told her brother, her eyes shining with pride. "He was so brave, Steven. You should have seen him. He saved my life."

"Good old Todd, the knight in shining armor," Jessica joked.

Elizabeth nodded seriously. To Elizabeth, Todd *was* a hero.

Just then the doorbell rang. Mr. Wakefield answered it, then returned to the living room with Todd at his side. In an instant Elizabeth was in his arms. As they embraced Elizabeth's parents tactfully left the room. Steven followed, dragging Jessica, who was not so tactful, behind him.

"I couldn't stay away any longer," Todd murmured, his arms tightening around Elizabeth. "I'm sorry I couldn't come home with you straight from the police station."

"It worked out fine," Elizabeth promised him. "I needed to talk to my family and you needed to talk to your dad."

They sat on the couch holding hands. For a long moment they looked deep into each other's eyes. It felt so right to be together again. Their closeness seemed all the more precious because they had come so near to losing it forever.

Elizabeth touched Todd's lips with her own. They shared a deep, warm kiss. Then they leaned back against the couch, wrapped cozily in each other's arms.

"I think I have most of the story figured out," Elizabeth said, "between Kevin's confession and all that Jessica told me just now, including what you'd told Aaron and Winston about the mugging and the trial in Burlington. I have only one question."

"What is it?" asked Todd.

"Why didn't you tell us? Why didn't you tell

me? About Kevin, I mean. About his past. Why did you keep such a terrible secret to yourself for so long?"

Todd laughed ironically. "I didn't tell you because I was trying to protect you."

"Trying to protect me?" Elizabeth questioned.

For a moment Todd was silent. Then he took a deep breath. Elizabeth sensed that it was hard for him to say what he was about to say. "Kevin threatened me. He swore that if I revealed anything about his past, he'd hurt someone I cared about. And he knew that the person I cared about most was you. That's why I didn't say anything," he concluded simply.

Elizabeth was too moved to speak. All the time that Todd was being reticent and distant, she thought it meant he didn't love her anymore. Instead, rather than loving her too little, he'd loved her too much.

"I was so torn," Todd said, his voice rough with emotion. "I knew Kevin was no good, that he was still pretty disturbed. I knew he could commit another crime, and he did. More than one. But I also knew that he'd make good on his threat to harm you. I couldn't risk telling anyone what I knew." Todd buried his face in Elizabeth's hair. "If anything had happened to you, Liz, I would never have forgiven myself."

Elizabeth held Todd close. She understood how divided Todd must have been. "Promise, though," she urged, "that you'll never keep anything so important from me again. We have to be honest with each other, about everything. I could have helped you."

"I know," Todd said.

"Because I would always support you," Elizabeth continued. "I believe in you."

Todd looked at her, his eyes warm with love and gratitude. "Knowing that makes it a lot easier to believe in myself."

"You *should* believe in yourself," Elizabeth declared. "Always. Don't ever stop, even for a minute."

"My father was just telling me the same thing," Todd said.

"Did you two get everything straightened out?"

Todd nodded. "I'm lucky, you know that, Liz?"

"It's funny," she mused. "How your family can shape you. I wonder if Kevin would have turned out differently if he'd ever felt that his parents really loved him."

"I don't know. Maybe. I can relate to him in a way. Dad was trying to shape me, and I went along with him. I wanted to be the kind of son *he* wanted. But in the end, it's still up to you to make your own choices, to be your own person," Todd said with conviction. "Kevin has taught me that."

"You're right. Kevin had problems at home, but ultimately no one else was responsible for his choices," Elizabeth agreed.

"Right. Maybe my dad was pressuring me to

work at Varitronics, but it was my choice either to go along with him or not. And maybe Kevin was threatening me, but I was still responsible for my own behavior. I made the wrong choice. I gave in to him and kept quiet. I'll know better next time."

They sat quietly for a few minutes. Then Elizabeth laughed. "In all this serious discussion, we're forgetting the most important thing."

Todd raised his eyebrows. "What's that?"

"That we're together again," Elizabeth said simply. "I love you, Todd."

Elizabeth and Todd's reunion had been interrupted by the ringing of the telephone. It was Aaron, calling from the Dairi Burger. All the Secca Lake day camp counselors—Winston, Enid, Cara, Jill, Kyle, Ed, and even Melissa—were at the Dairi Burger and they wanted Todd, Elizabeth, and Jessica to join them.

Todd was nervous as he and the twins drove downtown in the BMW. Because of Kevin's influence, Todd had alienated himself from the Fort Carroll and Big Mesa counselors. He'd even become estranged from his own Sweet Valley High friends. He supposed by now everyone knew what had happened that evening at the police station. They knew that Kevin, not Todd, was the mugger. But that didn't mean that things wouldn't still be strained between

Todd and the others. Particularly between Todd and Melissa. The last time Todd saw Melissa, she was under the impression that he had been her attacker. *What am I going to say to her?* Todd wondered as he parked the BMW in front of the Dairi Burger.

He wasn't kept in suspense for long. As he, Elizabeth, and Jessica entered the restaurant, they were greeted by a loud cheer.

The first person to speak was Melissa. "I'm sorry, Todd," she said simply. "I almost got you into pretty big trouble. I wish I'd known better, known *you* better. I wish I hadn't believed the things Kevin said about you. I'm sorry."

"I'm the one who's sorry," Todd corrected her.

"Can you forgive us for not giving you the benefit of the doubt?" asked Cara.

"We weren't very good friends," Winston said, his expression uncharacteristically solemn. "Because you were acting so hostile toward Kevin, we believed it when he told us he had something on you. It never occurred to us that *you* had something on *him!*"

"You had every reason to be suspicious of me," Todd assured them all. "I was acting pretty strangely. For a while, I was having some doubts about myself!"

"Never again, buddy," Aaron promised as they piled into a big booth at the back of the restaurant. "There'll never be any doubt in my mind about what kind of guy Todd Wilkins really is."

Across the booth, Todd met Elizabeth's eye. She smiled. "No more doubt in my mind, either," Todd said.

The most exciting stories ever in Sweet Valley history...

SWEET VALLEY HIGH

Celebrate the Seasons
with *SWEET VALLEY HIGH*
Super Editions

You've been a SWEET VALLEY HIGH fan all along—hanging out with Jessica and Elizabeth and their friends at Sweet Valley High. And now the SWEET VALLEY HIGH *Super Editions* give you more of what you like best—more romance—more excitement—more real-life adventure! Whether you're bicycling up the California Coast in PERFECT SUMMER, dancing at the Sweet Valley Christmas Ball in SPECIAL CHRISTMAS, touring the South of France in SPRING BREAK, catching the rays in a MALIBU SUMMER, or skiing the snowy slopes in WINTER CARNIVAL—you know you're exactly where you want to be—with the gang from SWEET VALLEY HIGH.

SWEET VALLEY HIGH SUPER EDITIONS

☐ 27650-6	AGAINST THE ODDS #51	$2.95
☐ 27720-0	WHITE LIES #52	$2.95
☐ 27771-5	SECOND CHANCE #53	$2.95
☐ 27856-8	TWO BOY WEEKEND #54	$2.99
☐ 27915-7	PERFECT SHOT #55	$2.95
☐ 27970-X	LOST AT SEA #56	$2.99
☐ 28079-1	TEACHER CRUSH #57	$2.95
☐ 28156-9	BROKEN HEARTS #58	$2.95
☐ 28193-3	IN LOVE AGAIN #59	$2.99
☐ 28264-6	THAT FATAL NIGHT #60	$3.25
☐ 28317-0	BOY TROUBLE #61	$2.95
☐ 28352-9	WHO'S WHO #62	$2.99
☐ 28385-5	THE NEW ELIZABETH #63	$2.99
☐ 28487-8	THE GHOST OF TRICIA MARTIN #64	$2.99
☐ 28518-1	TROUBLE AT HOME #65	$2.99
☐ 28555-6	WHO'S TO BLAME #66	$2.99
☐ 28611-0	THE PARENT PLOT #67	$2.99
☐ 28618-8	THE LOVE BET #68	$2.95
☐ 28636-6	FRIEND AGAINST FRIEND #69	$2.99
☐ 28767-2	MS. QUARTERBACK #70	$3.25
☐ 28796-6	STARRING JESSICA #71	$2.99
☐ 28841-5	ROCK STAR'S GIRL #72	$3.25
☐ 28863-6	REGINA'S LEGACY #73	$2.95